Perfectly
EVER
After

Perfectly EVER After

LOVE LESSONS BOOK THREE

ELIZABETH HAYLEY

WATERHOUSE PRESS

Copyright © 2019 Waterhouse Press, LLC
Cover Design by Waterhouse Press
Cover Images: Shutterstock

ISBN: 978-1-64263-242-2

Dedicated to all the Team Adam readers out there.

chapter one

"TALK DIRTY" — JASON DERULO

I'd never had a favorite time of day. I'd never given it a thought. But as I registered the smooth arm spread across my bare abdomen, the gentle rise and fall of the beautiful body that curled into mine, I chose. Mornings were now my favorite—as long as I was waking up next to Carly.

I tried to move so that I could see her more clearly, but my movement caused her to stir slightly, so I froze. She shifted closer to me, nuzzling herself into the crook of my arm. It amazed me how we fit together perfectly, like our bodies had been designed to lie beside each other in exactly this way.

I relaxed, deciding not to move so that she could sleep. I didn't get to wake up next to her often. Having a teenage daughter, I hadn't wanted to send the wrong message to Eva by moving in with a woman I wasn't married to, even though Carly and I had been together for two and a half years.

It was one thing for Eva to *think* Carly and I were having sex. But it was another thing entirely to confirm her suspicions by having Carly sleep over. By only spending the night together when Eva wasn't around, I hoped to maintain plausible deniability. And Carly understood. But in a week, I'd be spending every night with her because then Carly would become completely mine. She'd be Mrs. Adam Carter, and I vowed there in that bed that I would spend the rest of my life treasuring mornings with Carly.

My mom was having a girls' weekend with Eva so that Carly and I could finish some last-minute wedding stuff and enjoy our respective bachelor and bachelorette parties without having to worry about anything else. I couldn't wait to see what Frank had in store for me. Or maybe I could.

A hand skating down my stomach and disappearing below my comforter interrupted my thoughts. And as a slender finger leisurely trailed up my hardening cock, all thought left me completely.

"I didn't know you were awake." My voice was raspy with sleep and desire.

Carly pushed herself up and grinned into my neck. "I was." She wrapped her hand around my shaft and began to stroke, slowly at first, but quickly picked up speed as she squeezed me tighter.

A moan escaped my lips. *This solidifies it: mornings are definitely my favorite.*

She draped her leg over mine and began to rub her moist heat against my thigh. "Just think," she whispered, "one more week, and then we get to wake up this way every day."

I didn't tell her that just waking up next to her was enough for me. If she was willing to offer this erotic wake-up call daily, then far be it from me to dissuade her. "God, you make me so hard."

"And you make me wet. So wet, I think I may need to start

carrying an extra thong in my purse," she said breathlessly. "Do you want to feel how much you turn me on, Adam?"

I growled as I fluidly rolled my body so that I was on top of her. "You bet your sexy ass I do." I took her mouth firmly, running my tongue along the seam between her lips before she opened up and let my tongue delve inside. But I didn't stay there long. I had more pressing business farther south. I trailed kisses down her neck and then turned my attention to her perfectly round tits. "We're sleeping naked for the rest of our lives," I mumbled. "I like having complete access to you." I sucked a hardened nipple into my mouth, causing her back to bow off the bed.

She buried her hand in my hair. "Jesus Christ, you make my whole body feel like a live wire. Every time your lips are on my skin, I buzz everywhere. It's so good, baby." She moaned the words, causing pre-come to leak from my tip.

I began working my way lower, licking, nipping, and sucking my way down her flat stomach, over her hip bones, and finally arriving at my destination. I pushed a finger into her and was rewarded with Carly's mewling. I added a second finger and began working her toward release.

"I need your tongue, Adam. Please." Her grip on my hair tightened, and the entire scene was such a fucking turn-on, I almost came on the spot.

I kept moving my fingers inside her and leaned forward, darting my tongue out to make brief contact with her clit.

"Oh, shit. Do that again."

I smiled at how demanding she was. It was so sexy to be with a woman who knew exactly what she wanted. And who wasn't afraid to ask for it.

"You want it again? You want me to lick your pussy?"

"You bet your sexy ass I do," she said, returning the same words I'd just said to her.

She wore a seductive smile. "Open your eyes, Carly. I want you to watch what I do to you."

She opened them immediately, the blue orbs locking on me. She looked at me with so much love and primal need, my body instantly heated even more.

Keeping my eyes on her, I nuzzled between her legs, using my tongue to slip between her swollen folds before making contact with her clit again. But I didn't pull away this time. My tongue ravaged her, loving the taste of her sweet wetness in my mouth. Nothing tasted better than an aroused Carly. Nothing.

"Fuck, Adam, I'm so close."

I doubled my efforts, pumping my fingers into her at a maddening pace as I licked her like she were a melting popsicle.

I felt her body tense, her legs lock, and her shoulders lift off the mattress. Her whimpers grew louder. She was almost there when the sound of the doorbell interrupted our moans.

We both froze.

Carly fell back against the mattress. "Tell me that was *not* the doorbell."

We listened intently, but heard nothing. I was just about to tell her it was a false alarm and get back to the matter at hand when we heard it again.

"Who the hell could that be?" I couldn't keep the anger out of my voice. I was on the verge of giving the love of my life a mind-blowing orgasm, and now, instead of getting her off, I was getting up to answer the fucking door.

"Shit. What time is it?" Carly asked as she jumped from the bed and started throwing clothes on.

It really is a fucking crime to cover up her body. "Ten thirty. Why?"

"Damn it. I didn't realize it was so late. It's the girls downstairs."

I looked at her, confused, as I pulled on a pair of sweatpants and a T-shirt. "Why are the girls here already?"

"They have the whole day planned. Evidently I need a full day of pampering to beautify me before I'll be ready for my bachelorette party," she replied, giggling.

"Well, the joke's on them. You're beautiful without anyone else's help."

Carly darted her eyes over to me. The heat in them almost made me yell out the window and tell her friends to come back in an hour. Maybe two. She sauntered over to me in just panties and a pink ribbed tank top. When she reached me, she put her hands on my chest and pushed them back until her arms wrapped around my neck. "Do you have any idea how much I love you?" The sincerity in her words made my cock harden again.

I put my hands around her narrow waist and rested them on her ass. "If it's anywhere close to how much I love you, then I probably have a pretty good idea." I lowered my lips to hers, getting lost in the kiss and wishing it would never end.

The damn doorbell sounded again, ruining another intimate moment. I sighed and dropped my head to her shoulder. "I'll get the door while you finish getting dressed." I pulled away from her, though it took great effort, and headed downstairs.

"Be nice to them," Carly yelled. "They didn't mean to cock block."

I laughed at her comment and pulled open the front door. And after seeing eight eyes staring back at me, I simply moved back from the door and gestured up the steps.

They all piled in and flew up the stairs. I shook my head, closed the door, and made my way to the kitchen to brew some coffee. And as I leaned against the counter and waited for my jolt of caffeine to be ready, I couldn't help but think of how an orgasm would've been a much more effective way to wake up.

❤

The girls had rushed past me about twenty minutes later, Carly leaning in quickly to push a kiss to my lips. And as she was hustled out the door, she turned, told me to "behave," and shot me a wink.

After the herd left, I slowly climbed the stairs, wondering the entire way if I should climb back into bed and get a few more hours of sleep, or take a shower and get the day rolling. Walking into my bedroom, I glanced at the clock by my bed. Just after eleven o'clock. *Fuck it. Might as well get moving.*

I grabbed my cell phone, walked into my master bathroom, and shucked my clothes. As I leaned in to turn on the water and adjust the temperature to the hottest my skin would be able to stand without blistering, my phone chirped, alerting me that I had a text. I couldn't hold back my smile as I read the words.

You better wait up for me tonight. You and I have some unfinished business to tend to. I love you.

I quickly typed my reply.

I'd wait up for days if it meant getting to finish what we started this morning. Love you too.

I clicked my phone to sleep and stepped into the hot spray, hoping like hell my hard-on went away by the time Frank and the guys showed up.

❤

I spent the rest of my day getting ahead on some work that needed my attention before we left on our honeymoon. It was a welcome diversion since it was nearly impossible to maintain an erection while mapping out floor plans and running cost analyses. At a quarter after six, I decided I might as well go up and get ready for the evening ahead.

The guys all decided to meet at Frank's so that they could fill coolers with beer and do whatever other corny shit they had planned. Then, the luxury bus they'd rented would bring them to my place to pick me up around seven o'clock. We had eight fifteen dinner reservations at Gibson's Steakhouse in the city, and then the details became fuzzy. Frank had been very covert ops about what he had planned, though any idiot could guess that it would involve strippers and liquor.

Carly was aware that, with Frank running the show, literally anything was possible. She had assured me that the night was mine to have fun with my boys. *But* there were a few restrictions: my dick was to stay in my pants, I was to keep my mouth far away from anyone else's, and that if I got arrested, I'd have to let her know immediately but would spend the night in jail because she wasn't going to cut her night short to bail me out.

I figured these were reasonable and reminded her that what applied to me, applied to her. Except that she needed to keep dicks *out* of her pants.

I pulled out my dark rinse jeans and chose my favorite gray button-down. I rolled up the sleeves since I was sure the bus would be hot with fifteen dudes getting rowdy on it. Then I ran some gel through my hair, allowing it to rise into a slight fauxhawk. Once I was satisfied that I looked sufficiently badass for a guy in his mid-thirties, I grabbed my cell and wallet and headed downstairs to wait for the guys.

I wasn't waiting long when I heard a pounding on my door followed by Frank's obnoxious voice. "Open up, pussy. It's time to blow the roof off this motherfucker."

Blow the roof off this motherfucker? What grown man talks like that? I got my answer when I pulled open my door to see Frank standing there with a Corona in his hand, wearing a gold chain and sunglasses. At night.

"You're quite the nineties cliché." I shook my head at the sight of my oldest friend and best man.

"What do you mean?" Frank looked down at himself, running a hand over his black sweater, which he covered with a black leather jacket.

"Nothing," I replied with a laugh. "We all ready to leave?"

"I was born ready," he said as he started back toward the bus.

Rolling my eyes, I pulled the door shut behind me and locked it as I followed Frank toward the bus, silently hoping that none of the other guys were dressed like MTV reality show rejects.

I boarded the bus to hoots and hollers from my League of Unextraordinary Gentlemen. Thankfully, I quickly noticed that the rest of them were all dressed normally.

"There he is. Man of the hour," my friend Clay yelled as he thrust a beer into my hand.

I shook hands with my friends as I made my way to the back of the bus where Troy and Doug were sitting with Frank. "So the girls let all you guys off your leashes tonight, huh?" I joked.

"Just you wait." Doug laughed. "The first couple years after you get married, that fucker is like a choke collar. It loosens when she finally realizes she can't stand you and actually hopes you run away."

We busted out in raucous laughter, though I didn't see that happening with Carly and me. And while I was sure every engaged couple felt that way—that their love was different from all others—I knew what I had with Carly would never diminish. I'd want her forever.

The bus was loud as we all fought to be heard over one another. We recounted stories from the past, everyone having a tale to tell since I had met each of them at a different point in my life. I was actually surprised at how well they all got along, considering many of them didn't know each other very well, if at all.

We pulled up to Gibson's at eight after hitting the moderate traffic we had anticipated. Frank made his way to the front of our group and announced our arrival to the hostess, who smiled pleasantly at him.

"Just give us a few moments. We're preparing your table right now."

"No sweat, sweetheart. Take all the time you need." His response was off-putting enough in itself, but when he threw in a wink at the end, I grabbed him by the arm and pulled him back into the group.

"Take it easy, creepy Casanova," I murmured.

Frank looked affronted. "Whadaya mean? I was just talking to her about the table."

"Listen, it's bad enough that you're dressed like Heavy D. Can you try to not make every woman you encounter reach for her pepper spray?"

Frank scoffed. "Please, chicks dig the attention." Then he walked away from me, as though *I* were the crazy one.

Troy leaned toward me. "You're the one who made him the best man. You have only yourself to blame for what happens tonight." He chuckled loudly as he clapped a hand against my shoulder.

"Just promise me one thing," I said seriously, turning toward him. "When this ship starts to sink, save yourself." We both laughed, and I was glad I wasn't the only one who found Frank's behavior over the top.

"Okay, we're ready for you now," the hostess said sweetly.

"Oh, you better—"

"Frank," I warned, and he wisely let his sentence go unfinished.

We followed her back to a secluded section of the restaurant that could accommodate our large party.

After our drinks were ordered, we talked about nothing of much importance. In fact, the rest of dinner passed that way as well.

Finally, after we were all stuffed to the max, Frank stood up and cleared his throat.

Shit. Frank had sat at the other end of the table, and I hadn't heard much from him during dinner, which I hoped meant he had calmed down a little. But that hope began to fade as I heard him yell, "Shut up, you assholes."

The table fell silent, and we all looked at him expectantly.

"Now I've known Adam since we were kids. And over the years—"

"Save the speech for the wedding," Braden yelled.

"Shut up, dickhead," Frank growled. "Now as I was saying, over the years, I've seen a lot of women come and go in Adam's life. Well, maybe not *a lot* of women. You're pretty lame, you know that?"

I mumbled a "Fuck you," and picked up my beer.

"Anyway, there wasn't a single woman you dated who was ever good enough for you and Eva. Not a single one who made you truly happy. Until Carly. I'm glad you found her, man. Now you better hurry up and get that ring on her finger before she realizes what a douche you are," he said with a sly grin. "So let's raise our glasses to Adam and one of his last nights as a single man."

The guys lifted their drinks for the toast. I smiled at Frank, who grinned back at me. For as crazy as the man could get, he had had my back since we were in elementary school. And his support had never wavered once in all the years I'd known him. He didn't always seem like it, but Frank was a good friend.

"Now let's get drunk and grab some tits."

I quickly looked around, hoping the other diners hadn't heard Frank's declaration of debauchery. Draining my beer, I stood up to follow the group to the bus as I thought about how there was only one set of tits I wanted my hands on tonight. And I certainly wasn't going to find them wherever Frank was taking me. At least I hoped not.

❤

Our first stop was Jezebel's, one of the nicer gentlemen's clubs in the city. It had a liquor license, so we didn't need to cart the beer cooler inside. Frank had evidentially told them we were coming, because we didn't need to pay the cover before being let inside.

We lasted fifteen minutes.

"If they don't like dirty talk, they should choose a different profession," Frank charged.

"Dude, no chick wants to be asked if she can deep-throat a cucumber." Charlie sighed in frustration.

"It was a serious question," Frank argued.

"How the hell does Claire put up with you? You have the maturity of a twelve-year-old," Troy declared.

"Please, I'm the best thing that ever happened to her," Frank said, trying to maintain a straight face, but failing miserably.

"Right, some prize," I countered before turning to Troy and answering his question. "And he doesn't act this way when Claire is around because she'd kick his ass up and down Broad Street."

"I get one night of freedom like every five years, for fuck's sake. I'll be damned if I'm not going to enjoy it." Frank pouted as we boarded the bus and set off for our next stop.

Oh, he's got to be kidding. I looked out the window as the bus pulled to a stop and took in the run-down building lit up by a gaudy neon sign.

"Are we really stopping at The Magic Shop?" I nearly whined. This place was notorious for dirty deeds and skanky strippers. I was pretty sure you could catch gonorrhea just from sitting on the stools.

"We sure are." Frank's eyes were bright, his excitement evident by the way he pushed himself to the front of the bus and hopped off.

A couple of the guys grabbed the beer cooler and followed Frank off the bus.

I looked over at Doug, who simply shrugged and started off the bus. Finally, I rubbed a hand over my face and followed my friends toward the building.

Again, we were let right in and directed to a roped-off section to the left of the center stage. I briefly looked up at the girl currently dancing on the pole. She looked young but weathered, like she'd been ridden hard and put away wet. Her stomach had stretch marks, probably from the children she was up there trying to support.

This was why I hated places like this. At the nicer establishments, you could convince yourself that the girls were all students trying to pay their way through med school. A brighter life was just a lap dance away for them. But the women here had no other choice. They danced to survive, and it was damned depressing.

I slunk back into my chair, trying to look anywhere but at the completely naked woman on the stage. It felt... wrong to ogle her. Not that the prospect of doing so was all that appealing anyway.

I spent the next twenty minutes making conversation with my friends in the hopes of avoiding any of the topless women who tried to get close to me. It didn't help my effort that Frank kept pointing to me and tucking money in their G-strings. Just as I was beginning to think that the girls had gotten the hint that I didn't want their attention, I was proven dead wrong.

"All right, gentlemen, it's time for our ladies to show one particular man what he'll be missing after he gets married next weekend."

The announcer's voice caused my entire body to seize. *They better not be talking about me.*

"So come up on stage, Adam, and get your punishment for making the biggest mistake of your life."

The announcer laughed at his joke, but I didn't see the humor. He was obviously insinuating that my getting married was a mistake. But the only mistake I'd made was agreeing to come into this hovel. Well, that and allowing Frank to plan my bachelor party. No way was I going up on stage. Nope. Nah-uh.

"Get up there, Adam," Frank yelled with a big shit-eating grin on his face.

I'm going to fucking kill him.

"Come on, big guy," Troy added. "It's a rite of passage."

I looked up at the stage where two women, one in some sort of cheap Catwoman suit and the other in a policewoman getup, were waiting on me to join them. *There is no place on this earth where I would willingly walk* toward *those two.*

Though it quickly became evident that I wasn't being given a ton of free will in this instance anyway. Doug, Frank, and Brian all flanked me and forcibly pulled me from my chair. I had never wanted to stay seated on an STD-infested chair so badly in my life.

Once they had me standing, the bastards lifted me up on stage. The other patrons-slash-sex-offenders were cheering me on as my former band of brothers started chanting my name. Even up on stage, I made no move to get closer to the girls. Sensing my hesitation, Catwoman decided to take things into her own hands, because she strutted toward me, grabbed the front of my shirt, and yanked me to the chair that had been set up on stage.

I knew a lot of things in that moment. I knew I wanted to be virtually anywhere but there. I knew Frank was an asshole. I knew these two women were horrifying on almost every level, and I knew that Carly was most definitely having a better evening than me. But the knowledge that trumped all others was that I absolutely, unequivocally, beyond a shadow of a doubt did *not* want to sit in that semen-crusted chair.

But as Catwoman backed me up against it, the X-rated female rent-a-cop reached up from behind me, grabbed my shoulders, and forced me down. Had I been expecting her to touch me, I would've been prepared to resist. Even though she was built like an offensive lineman, I definitely would've been able to remain standing against her assault. But I hadn't been ready, so there I sat, practically able to *feel* the blood-borne pathogens scurrying into my body.

"You like playing hard to get?" the naughty policewoman asked.

"Oh, I'm not playing, ladies. Trust me." I didn't *want* to be a dick. I knew they were only doing what they'd been paid to do. But I just couldn't help it.

"You're being a very bad boy by not doing what you're told," Catwoman said seductively. Well, as seductive as someone who probably smoked two packs of Newports a day could sound.

"Uh, sorry?" I was willing to try anything by that point. Maybe contrite was the way to play it.

"Too late," Catwoman pouted as Kojak handcuffed me to the chair.

"You've gotta be fucking kidding me," I murmured as I pulled on the handcuffs, hoping they were as flimsy as everything else in this place so that I could break free.

"What should we do to him, boys?" Catwoman shouted.

My dickhead friends started yelling all kinds of shit, but I was too busy debating whether or not to chew off my own hand to process any of it.

"I think we should start with a whipping," Kojak offered with a sly grin.

I think we should most definitely not *start with that.*

"Great idea," Catwoman agreed.

"You know, that's probably *not* a great idea," I started to explain.

"Shut up," Catwoman yelled as she grabbed my shirt again and pulled it firmly, causing buttons to scatter.

I sat there in utter disbelief, my shirt ruined because some beauty school dropout was on a power trip. *Fuck this.* "I hope you made at least fifty dollars in tips tonight, because that's what you owe me for my shirt." As soon as the words left my mouth, I wished I could have taken them back. It wasn't these girls' fault that my best man was a complete asshole. But my outburst only made me more uncomfortable, which was shocking because I didn't think anything said discomfort more than being shackled to a chair while being stripped in front of strangers. "You need to let me up. Please." I gritted through the "please," hoping they would have mercy on me.

"And you need to shut the fuck up and let us do what we've been paid to do," Catwoman hissed.

Great, now she's really going to kick my ass.

"Get his belt," Catwoman ordered Kojak.

Kojak walked in front of me. Then she suddenly pushed her tits in my face and let her body slide down mine until she was kneeling in front of me. Her hands went to my belt, and I nearly tipped the chair over backward trying to get away from her. But they were clearly used to having men wrench back to avoid their touch, because Catwoman had braced herself behind me, preventing my chair from falling.

Kojak loosened my belt and pulled it from my pants. She then handed it to Catwoman, who circled me like a predator stalking its prey.

"If you hit me with that belt, I'll have you arrested for

assault," I warned. I didn't really mean the words, but said them anyway, praying like hell they would be enough to deter her.

She smirked at me. "Wouldn't be the first time, and it certainly won't be the last." And with that, she reared back with my belt and then let it fly forward.

It took me a moment to register the pain. I was too stunned that I'd actually just been hit with my own belt. But a sharp sting soon flared across my chest. And as if that wasn't bad enough, Kojak came out of nowhere, yanked up my undershirt, and licked the welt that had formed.

That was the point I officially lost my mind. I began to buck wildly, causing the girls to fling themselves backward. This, coupled with the rage-infused insults I was hurling at everyone in the place, caused Frank to rush the stage and get the handcuff key from Kojak.

Once I was free, I stood up, told Frank he owed me a new shirt, jumped off stage, and got the hell out of there. I boarded the bus and checked my cell phone. *A text from Carly. Thank God.*

She had sent me a picture of her sitting on a red vinyl couch, sipping her drink, with her dress inched suggestively up her leg. She looked fucking beautiful, and I knew in that moment that I wanted—no *needed*—to be wherever she was. My traitorous friends boarded the bus soon after me, and everyone found a seat as we pulled out of the parking lot.

There was a few minutes of tense silence, until Frank asked, "So where to now?"

I glared at him with such contempt, I thought he would wither and die on the spot. "If you take me anywhere but home, I swear I will make your wife a widow tonight."

Frank looked at me for a moment before silently standing and conveying our destination to the driver.

I spent the rest of the ride home staring out the window, wondering if it was too late to find a new best man. *The mailman has always been friendly. Maybe he's a good choice.*

When the bus pulled up outside my house, I darted out of my seat and practically sprinted to my front door.

I heard Frank's voice behind me. "You had a good time, right, Adam?"

I ignored him as I put my key in the lock.

"Adam?"

The lock turned and I threw the door open.

"Adam!"

I turned long enough to shoot the bus the finger before slamming the door.

I looked down at my watch: one in the morning. Odds were that Carly wasn't home yet, but that didn't stop me from taking the steps two at a time to check. I ran into my bedroom only to find it empty. *No problem. This just gives me time to prepare.*

I shed my clothes and headed into the bathroom, wanting to rid myself of the stench that permeated the air in The Magic Shop. I inspected myself in the mirror. The swelling had gone down, turning my welt into a nasty bruise. *Fucking animals.*

I jumped in the shower and lathered my body with soap. Twice. Then I quickly dried off and made my way back into the bedroom, wearing only a towel around my waist. Trying to insert some romance into this seedy evening, I lit a couple of candles, lost the towel, and climbed into bed to wait for the one woman whose touch could undo everything I had endured.

But as the minutes ticked by, and two o'clock became two

thirty, I was having a nearly impossible time staying awake. Finally, at a quarter to three, my phone chirped. Expecting a text from Carly to tell me she was on her way, I was more than a little disappointed to see that it was from a number I didn't recognize. But my disappointment only grew as I read the words.

Hey Adam. It's Corinne. Carly is WASTED and passed out on my couch. So, we decided to leave her there, and we'll just bring her home in the morning. Hope you're enjoying your night!

I closed my eyes and counted to ten. Very. Slowly. I resisted the urge to ask Corinne where she lived so I could pick Carly up and bring her home. Even if all I got to do was hold her, that would have been better than lying there alone all night. But I knew that would only make me seem like a lunatic, so I texted a brief *Thanks* and threw my phone on my bedside table.

And just before I drifted off into one of the most restless sleeps of my life, I swore to myself that I would make it my mission in life to keep Eva off the pole.

chapter two

The days after my bachelor party were more insane. In my defense, not ever having a wedding before had made it difficult to predict what all the chaos would be like. And since Carly had organized each detail gradually along the way, I figured that the week before the actual wedding would be relatively calm. Everything was done, right?

Wrong. Somehow, Carly had caught a few last-minute issues with the flowers and her dress. And it wasn't like I was marrying Bridezilla. These were real problems that needed to be rectified, and since the wedding was being held at a lodge in the Poconos a few hours away, it made it difficult to oversee all the small details.

Carly caught the first mishap when she went to try on her dress. I'm not sure why women need to have a million dress fittings in the last few weeks leading up to the wedding. I mean how much could your body change in a few days? But when Carly went to pick up her dress for the last time, it was two sizes too big. Unless I wanted my wife's tits popping out as we said our vows, that was a huge issue. It turned out that they had put another woman's alterations on Carly's dress.

I assured her that her dress would be fixed and that none of the little things mattered in the big picture. As long as we were married at the end of the day—and her boobs managed to stay tucked away until I got my hands on them later—the day itself would be relatively insignificant. But regardless of my assurance, Carly checked and double-checked every detail, no matter how minor.

Apparently, fall weddings called for darker flowers. Who knew? And since we'd be getting married in the middle of November, Carly had chosen some flowers that matched the deep red of the bridesmaids' dresses. But when she called the florist in the mountains near the lodge, they'd forgotten to add the bouquet that she planned to toss and the flowers for the centerpieces had been the wrong color.

When she set the phone down on the kitchen counter, I could see the tears starting to form. It wasn't like her. The stress of the wedding had clearly taken a toll on her. "It'll all work out. I promise," I said, pulling her into me and stroking her hair as she rested her head on my chest.

"I know. I just want it to all go smoothly. I'll be happy when it's all over and I can have you to myself in Jamaica for a week."

A small laugh escaped me before I replied, "A week in Jamaica? Right now, I'd settle for about fifteen minutes in this kitchen."

She glanced down at her watch. "What do ya know? We've got fifteen minutes."

I felt my cock stiffen instantly at the thought. Eva wouldn't be home from basketball practice for almost another half hour. Somehow, over the past week, Carly and I had made a few attempts to have sex, but we could never seem to finish what we'd started. Life just kept getting in the way. But there we were, alone in our kitchen and hornier than all hell. Well, at least *I* was.

I urgently brought my mouth to hers, and I relished the feel of her body against mine as I backed her roughly against the counter. She moaned softly and let her head fall to the side, allowing me access to the sensitive flesh on her neck. I felt my pulsing erection jerk against my jeans, and I circled my hips against her for a few moments before pulling back enough to slip a hand up her shirt to thumb her nipples beneath her bra.

"Oh, Adam, I've wanted this all day."

"Yeah? What is it you've wanted? Tell me." I loved to hear her talk to me, and since our first intimate encounter—not counting the one in ninth grade—had begun under the pretense that we wouldn't see each other again, we'd both been uninhibited. Thankfully, that attitude had continued once we'd started dating.

"To feel your cock in my hand," she said as she stroked me above my pants, causing me to nearly explode on contact. "Your fingers inside me."

At her words, I slid my hand from her breast down beneath her underwear. I groaned as my hand hit her pussy. *Jesus, she's fucking soaked.* Her heavy breaths faltered as I thrust two fingers deep inside her. "Like this?" I asked, already knowing the answer, but wanting her to confirm it anyway.

"God, Adam, exactly like that."

I felt myself get harder with every stroke of her palm above my jeans, and I was so fucking close to coming. "You want me to make you come like this?" She moaned in agreement, and I felt like I might lose it at any moment as she rubbed her hand against my hard-on more vigorously. "God, Carly, you're gonna make me come in my pants."

"That's kinda the idea."

Shit, that's hot. With great effort, I tried to hold my orgasm off, but it was nearly impossible after how tense this week had been. Combining the stress of the wedding with the sexual tension we'd been experiencing since the day of the bachelor and bachelorette parties, and we were both long overdue for a release.

"Come for me, Carly. I can't wait much longer." Just as I said the words, Carly's phone vibrated on the counter next to us, stealing our attention for a brief moment. "Leave it," I instructed, sensing she was tempted to answer.

Her hand left my cock for a moment to look at the screen of her phone. "It's the florist, Adam. I gotta take this."

"No, you don't. The only thing you have to take was in your hand a few seconds ago."

Carly shot me a playful look. "We'll finish this later. I promise."

I removed my hand from her pants and let out a deep sigh of frustration as I looked down at how hard I was and realized Eva would be home soon. *Fuck. Me.*

❤

Needless to say, Eva had come home before Carly had been able to make good on her promise, so I didn't get much sleep that night. I tried to think of anything that would stave off the arousal I'd been feeling. I ran through the pre-wedding to-do list in my mind, hoping the thoughts would occupy my brain enough to focus on something other than how hard I'd been for most of the night.

Okay, pack the car, make sure things are set for the rehearsal dinner when we arrive at the hotel, meet that asshole Frank and the other guys in his room at ten in the morning to get ready for the wedding, see Carly walk down the aisle in a white dress, then rip it off her that night. Fuck, this isn't working.

Hadn't Carly seen those commercials that warned about the dangers of having an erection that lasted more than four hours? Obviously, she had no concern for my well-being. I'd texted her around eleven, trying to get a little verbal foreplay started, but she said she still needed to pack and she'd see me tomorrow. And also this . . .

Try to get some sleep. And don't even think of touching yourself. It'll be so much better when I can do that for you.

Shit. Why had I agreed to that? And why did I feel like she'd know if I did it anyway? For whatever reason, I felt a promise was a promise, and I didn't want to break any promise I made to her before our wedding day, no matter how insignificant.

chapter three

"GIRLS JUST WANT TO HAVE FUN" — CYNDI LAUPER

I wasn't entirely sure why Carly and her sister had declared my house as wedding central, but by Thursday, I was overrun with wedding crafts. As I watched them tying ribbons around our wedding favors, I knew that I couldn't fight it. Shit was *everywhere*. Paper was strewn all over the floor from their catastrophic attempt at making programs for the ceremony— an attempt they abandoned after two hours of arguing and then finally declaring that programs were a waste of their precious time.

I walked over to the French doors that led onto the patio and stared out, a frown settling over my features.

"They're fine, Adam." Carly's voice was filled with an amusement I didn't share.

"Did you see his arm? He has a tattoo for Christ's sake. What sixteen-year-old kid has a tattoo?"

"A lot of them probably," she replied casually, seeming unperturbed by the fact that my daughter's boyfriend had ink that would make him fit right in when he eventually went to prison for knocking over a liquor store.

"I hate him."

I heard Carly set the wedding favor down. "That's very mature."

"It's also very true," I retorted. "Maybe he's preparing his body for the numerous other tattoos he'll receive in cellblock eight," I added, voicing my previous thoughts.

Katie snorted. "I told you we should've gotten tattoos on the night of your bachelorette party, Carly. Maybe you would've made more friends that night."

I almost ignored Katie's words, but they sank in after a few seconds had lapsed. "Wait...what?" I turned around to face them. Carly's face paled, and she shot a deadly glare at her sister.

Katie looked confused. "What?"

"Why would having a tattoo have made Carly more friends?"

"Oh, shit." Katie's eyes darted cautiously to Carly. "You didn't tell him, did you?"

"No. Not yet," Carly replied icily.

Katie jumped up from the floor. "Man, you know what? I am *super* thirsty. I think I'm just going to go get a drink. Can I get anyone one? No? Great. See ya in a few." She practically sprinted from the room as Carly and I stared at one another.

Finally, I couldn't take the silence anymore. "I'm not going to like this, am I?"

"That depends."

"On what?"

"If you're in a good mood or not." Carly cracked a slight smirk, probably hoping to lessen the tension that had enveloped the room.

I just looked at her, letting her know that any good mood that had been present had vanished.

She sighed before standing and walking toward me, though stopping a few feet away. "Remember when Corinne texted to tell you I was passed out on her couch last Saturday?"

I simply nodded.

"Well, that may have been a lie." Carly winced as she spoke, as if saying the words had hurt her.

My shoulders squared, and I shoved my hands in my pockets. Tension radiated through my body. I could handle a lot of things. Lying wasn't one of them. "So what's the truth?"

Carly's eyes flashed to the floor before she brought them back up to my face. "I may have gotten arrested."

My jaw dropped in shock. *Arrested? Is this a fucking joke?*

"It's pretty funny really," she continued.

I straightened again, almost challenging her to make it even remotely funny.

"I was really drunk, Adam. I only remember bits and pieces of what happened."

"I'm sure your friends have filled in the gaps by now," I replied tersely.

"Yeah, they have," she said shyly. "Okay, here it goes. We were walking through the city, heading to another bar, when we passed one of those horse-drawn carriages. The driver wasn't around, so I decided to climb up in his seat so the girls could take my picture."

"That's it? You were arrested for that?" Disbelief dripped from my mouth with the words.

"No. I was ... um ... arrested for operating a vehicle while intoxicated."

"What?" I yelled.

"I wanted the picture to look authentic, so I untied the horse's reins from where the driver had tied them and climbed into his seat. But then the stupid horse started to move. For the record, it's way harder to steer those things than it looks."

Her attempt at humor fell flat as I stared at her. "Are you for real right now?"

"Unfortunately, yes. The driver came running out, but the horse had already pulled me halfway down the block. Thank God those horses are trained to walk so slowly because the driver was able to catch up to us before we reached the intersection. But then he started screaming at me and making a huge scene, so a policeman stopped. And that's when I got arrested."

It was the most ridiculous story I had ever heard. And part of me wanted to laugh. But a bigger part of me was furious that this was the first I was hearing about it. "Why the hell didn't you tell me? You had your friends lie to me, Carly. Do you have any idea what that feels like? That my soon-to-be wife gets arrested and instead of calling for me to come help her, she lies to me about it instead?"

She moved closer to me and placed her hands on my chest. "I'm so sorry, Adam. I didn't even know they had lied to you until the next day. I was drunk and wasn't thinking straight."

"But you weren't drunk the next day. Or any of the other days between Saturday and today. But you still never told me. Were you *ever* going to be honest with me?" The anger was radiating off me. She knew how important honesty was to me, but she'd kept up the lie anyway.

"Yes, I swear I was going to tell you. But everything has been so crazy with the wedding, and I didn't want to infuse one more piece of drama into this week. And it really isn't a big deal. Once I sobered up, the police simply issued a ticket and told me to pay the fine. It won't even go on my permanent record. I think they found the whole thing pretty entertaining."

I was sure the look on my face informed her that I didn't agree with the cops' assessment of the situation. "You're wrong, Carly. This is a *very* big deal." I turned back toward the patio, not needing to see her to know that she understood why I was taking this so seriously. She was well aware of my past, and she also probably had a pretty good idea of how I'd react to the fact that she'd withheld this news. As I looked outside, seething, my body stiffened as I scanned the yard. "Where did Eva and Cage go?"

Carly moved to look around me. "I'm not sure."

Yanking the doors open, I stepped outside. "Eva? Eva, where are you?" No answer. I scanned the backyard for any sign of them, but saw nothing. When I walked back into the house, I began searching for them. I opened the basement door and yelled down. Nothing. I walked into the kitchen, but only found Katie nervously biting her nails. Finally, I walked over to the stairs and yelled up, "Eva, are you up there?"

I swung around quickly, figuring she couldn't be up there. But I jerked to a halt when I heard her reply.

"Eva, get down here right now," I demanded from the foot of the steps.

Seconds later, Eva sheepishly started down the stairs with that cocky punk right behind her. She stopped halfway down and leaned against the wall.

"Has everyone lost their goddamn minds today?" My voice was almost shrill. I took a calming breath before continuing. "You know you're not allowed to have boys in your room. What are you thinking?"

Eva's voice was quiet when she answered me. "We just went up there real quick because I had to recharge my phone."

"I'm really supposed to believe that? Come on, Eva. I wasn't born yesterday."

Eva looked affronted as she met my eyes, her own anger showing in hers. "It's the truth."

"That seems to be a novel concept in this house: truth. I'm starting to think no one is capable of it."

"Adam, that's enough. Maybe Cage should head home so that we can talk to Eva about this in private."

I flew around to face Carly, the words out of my mouth before I had time to think about them. "*We* don't need to do anything. *I* will talk to *my* daughter. Besides, I'm not sure your influence is really what's best for Eva right now."

Once I processed the words and registered the devastation on Carly's face, my senses returned. I had never wanted to take words back so badly in my life. "Shit, Carly, I didn't mean that."

"Save it, Adam. Katie," she called and waited for her sister to appear. "We're leaving."

Katie simply nodded and helped Carly gather her things before they headed out the door.

"Baby, please, don't go. Let me apologize," I begged, but to no avail. She walked out of my house without so much as a look back. I sighed heavily, still staring at the door. "Time for you to go too, Cage."

"Bye, Eva. I'll see you tomorrow." I thought I heard the little prick give Eva a kiss before he came down the steps and strutted out the front door. At least he had sense enough not to say a word to me.

I roughly pushed the door shut behind Cage as he left and just stood there for a few seconds, trying like hell to regain some control.

"Dad," Eva started.

"Don't," I warned without turning around. "Just go up to your room. You knew the rules, and you broke them. You're grounded. And if you argue with me, Eva, I swear, not only will Cage not be coming to the wedding, but you also won't see him at all."

All I heard was a huff from behind me before she stalked back up the stairs and slammed her door.

I shook my head, wondering how everything had gone to hell so quickly. But more importantly, I wondered how the hell I was going to fix it.

chapter four

"COLLIDE" — HOWIE DAY

I gave Carly enough time to get back to her apartment in the city before I called her. And when she didn't answer, I hung up and called again. And again. I finally left a voicemail the fourth time, explaining that I was sorry and for her to please call me. The fifth time I called, her phone went straight to voicemail, indicating that Carly had most likely turned the damn thing off.

I went up to bed early, weary from two of the most important women in my life being supremely pissed at me. But I didn't sleep. Tossing and turning all night, I thought about what I said to Carly and how unfair it had been. Though I couldn't help but ponder the ways she'd been unfair to me as well.

For me, this whole thing came down to trust—trust that we would be honest with each other, especially if one of us were in some kind of trouble. But Carly hadn't done that. She hadn't trusted me to know that she'd been arrested. I wondered what it was about our relationship that made her feel she couldn't come to me. And I worried that her reason was something fundamental to our lives together. Something we couldn't move forward without.

Thinking sucks.

I couldn't bring myself to delve into the Cage issue with Eva. It was something that would have to wait until after the wedding. *If* Carly was talking to me in time for us to *have* a wedding.

That thought jarred me more fully awake. I couldn't play these games. Refusing to lie there and wonder about where I stood with Carly for one more minute, I rolled out of bed. The clock next to me illuminated the time: almost three thirty. I quickly pulled on a pair of sweatpants and a hoodie and reached for a piece of paper and a pen so I could leave a note for Eva explaining where I'd gone.

I crept quietly down the hall and into Eva's room. I placed the note on the bedside table on top of her phone, knowing she'd see it there. As I turned around to leave, I couldn't help but stop and look at Eva's sleeping form for a moment. I rarely got to see her this way anymore: calm, relaxed, silent. I couldn't resist leaning down to place a gentle kiss on her cheek, just like I used to do after I tucked her in when she was a little girl.

I suddenly found myself overwhelmed with the speed at which time passed. And deciding not to waste another second, I quickly left the room and headed to Carly's.

❤

Finding a parking spot outside of Carly's building wasn't an easy feat. But after finally finding one a block and a half away, I hurried toward her apartment. I hadn't given much thought to what I was actually going to say once I got there, but I was sure something would come to me. Hopefully, it'd be the right something.

I punched in the code to enter and waved to George, the security officer who guarded her lobby.

"Late night, Mr. Carter?"

"One of the latest," I replied as I boarded the elevator and hit the button for the sixth floor.

When the elevator dinged, letting me know I had reached my destination, my stomach lurched slightly. The truth was, I had no clue how our talk would play out. And that scared the living fuck out of me.

I arrived at her door and stood there staring at it for a few moments, trying to calm my breathing and convince myself that going there had been a good idea. Finally, I rang the bell. Impatience washed through me, so I started firmly knocking on her door. "Carly? Baby, it's Adam. Can you open the door please? Carly?"

The door jerked open, and I found myself face-to-face with a still sleepy Carly, dressed in flannel pajama pants and a white tank top. Even mussed by sleep, she was still breathtaking.

"Adam?" she whispered, breaking my trance. "What are you doing here? It's four in the morning."

I let out a deep sigh. "I know. I'm sorry. I just..." I leaned against the doorjamb. "I just needed to talk to you. I don't like that you left. Why'd you walk away?" I was as surprised by my words as she seemed to be. That thought really hadn't entered my mind until that moment, but I recognized it as completely true. I was angry that she had walked out... on me.

"I just needed time to...think. I didn't walk away from *you*."

"Yes, you did. I get it. What I said was hurtful and totally out of line. But your first instinct was to leave. I need to know why."

Carly and I hadn't fought much during our time together, and when we had, it had been silly and superficial. The problem we encountered now was neither of those things, and I had no idea how to best handle it. Not to mention, the timing fucking blew.

"I didn't want to get into it in front of Eva," she finally responded, though her eyes shifted toward the floor, showing it for the flimsy excuse it was.

"I call bullshit."

Her eyes darted to mine, narrowing. She was getting pissed off, and that was just fine with me. Maybe anger would help the truth come out.

"You know what, Adam? Screw you. You don't get to barge in here after making me feel like crap this afternoon and call me a bullshitter. If I'd thought talking about it would've been beneficial in any way, I would've stayed. But it wouldn't have been, so I left." Carly was having no issue with eye contact anymore, her eyes boring into me with the ferocity of a wounded animal that had been backed into a corner.

"Why wouldn't talking have helped?" My tone conveyed the confusion I felt.

"Because you only hear what you want to. I tell you a story about being arrested and spending a night in jail, and instead of being concerned, you immediately start calling me a liar. And then Eva tries to explain herself, and you jump halfway down her throat. But my favorite is how I tried to help with Eva—who's supposed to be my stepdaughter as of tomorrow—and you trash me right in front of her."

I rubbed a hand over my face and tried to process her words. "Listen," I finally said, "I agree with you that I could've handled the whole jail thing better. And I am concerned. It was my concern that caused me to react that way. I don't like feeling out of control, especially about things that are so important to me. But I was a dick about it, and I'm sorry for that."

Her features slackened at my words, some of the irritation slipping away.

I continued, trying to get us back to where we'd been before the whole disaster started. "And I was wrong for what I said about you in front of Eva. You're a great role model. If I were concerned about having you around my daughter, then you wouldn't be. I'd love for her to be like you: strong, independent, successful." I started inching toward her as I spoke, watching her skin flush. "I love you, baby. I want to share my future with you. But there are some things that I do need to handle on my own." I was close to her now, but she quickly withdrew when she heard my last words.

"What things?"

"Huh?" I asked, leaning toward her again.

She took a large step back. "What things do you need to handle on your own?"

My head tilted in confusion. "Things with Eva."

She eyed me warily. "So, let me get this straight." She started to pace in front of me. "You're going to handle all things concerning Eva."

"Well, I . . . Why do I get the feeling you're going to make this into a big deal?"

"Because it *is* a big deal. We're supposed to be partners, Adam. In every way. But you're basically telling me that we aren't going to be. Eva is a huge part of your life, a part that you don't want me involved in. How is that not a big deal?"

I leaned back into the wall next to the still open door. "Carly, I don't mean for it to hurt you. It's just that . . . it's been just me and Eva for sixteen years. I don't know how to share the responsibility I feel toward her. I've never had to before."

"It's not about *having* to. It's about you *wanting* me to help you raise your daughter."

Her eyes welled with tears, and while I was sorry this was upsetting her, I didn't know how to fix it. "But she's virtually raised, Carly. In a year and a half, she'll be leaving for college. I've gotten her this far. I'm capable of getting her the rest of the way without any help."

I knew she wasn't implying that I hadn't done a good job as a father, but I couldn't help feeling that way anyway. Raising Eva had been difficult, but I had done a damn good job. And if I were being honest, part of me needed to finish what I'd started. I wanted the thrill of seeing Eva excel in life and be able to know that I had gotten her there with minimal outside help. *I* was responsible for the woman Eva would become. I didn't want to share that glory. I didn't feel anyone else deserved it.

Carly's tears fell, but she seemed oblivious to them, not even attempting to wipe them away.

She just didn't get it. "I'm not trying to hurt you, Carly," I said as I reached for her.

She shrank away from me. "Stop *saying* that. Especially since you clearly don't have to try. It seems to come pretty easily to you."

I dropped my hand, feeling as though the future of our relationship depended on this conversation. And I was fucking it all up. "When have I ever hurt you?"

"You're hurting me now," she whispered, looking away from me.

"That isn't my intention. I'd give my life for you. You have to know that." My voice was pleading, begging her to let us move on.

I noticed the slight lift of her shoulders, the straightening of her back. "We have a long day ahead of us. I just need some time to process everything. And I think *you* do too. We should probably get some sleep."

She was dismissing me, though I hoped not permanently. Maybe she was right. After some sleep, maybe we'd be able to see things more clearly.

"Okay." I leaned in and gave her a quick peck on the cheek. "I'll see you at noon?"

She wiped tears from her cheeks. "Yeah. I'll see you at noon."

I simply nodded before turning and heading home.

❤

I'd gotten home around five thirty, but falling back to sleep wasn't an option. So I puttered around the house instead, cleaning things that didn't need it, moving things that didn't need to be moved.

Eva had woken up at ten, and I'd made her breakfast: pancakes and bacon. A peace offering of sorts, which she accepted, though she grumbled while eating.

I eventually changed out of my sweats and into comfortable jeans and my favorite blue cable-knit sweater. Then I headed outside to load our luggage. It was difficult trying to maneuver everything because Eva's bags of God-knows-what took up about half of my mom's car. "Jeez, Eva, we're going to the mountains for a few nights, not a month-long journey up Mt. Everest. What did you bring?"

"Just girl stuff, Dad. God, do you have to know everything?"

"Yes," I replied stoically. "The answer to that will always be yes." Had this girl learned *nothing* about me in her sixteen years of life? For all I knew, she could have anything in there: grain alcohol, a brick of cocaine, a homemade bomb, a case of condoms. *Christ.* Why had I let myself think that last thought? I'd meant for all my internal guesses to be ridiculously implausible, but with that teenage Lothario coming to the wedding, the case of condoms hadn't seemed too farfetched. With a name like Cage, anything was possible.

I'd spoken to Eva about sex more times than I would have liked to. If I were being completely honest, one time had really been too many. And each time, she'd assured me that she wasn't sexually active. But my mind couldn't help but go there. She was going on seventeen and had been in a relationship with this guy for over five months.

Any good father would worry. And with a name that could come straight out of any of those romance novels Carly was always reading, I was certain Cage couldn't be trusted. I was thinking about how much I regretted allowing him to live after the whole debacle yesterday when Carly pulled up.

She wore her long red hair down, allowing it to flow over her light green sweater. *And... I'm hard.* I wondered if it would always be that way: one look at her and I'd be ready to throw her on the closest available surface and have my way with her. I hoped so.

She approached cautiously, confusion outlining her features. "Are we taking your mom's car to the Poconos?"

"No, she's just here to pick up Eva. I thought..." I shrugged shyly. "Maybe we could talk."

She gave me a brief nod before returning to her car to start unloading it. I followed her, taking the bags from her and carrying them to my car. I quickly threw them in the trunk, hugged my mom and Eva, and clapped my dad on the shoulder before they started off toward the mountains. "Ready to go?" I asked Carly with more energy than I actually had.

"Yup," she sighed and climbed into the passenger seat.

I exhaled a long breath. *This ride is going to suck ass.*

We were silent for a while, both of us looking out the window, pretending to be interested in anything but each other. Though her reason for doing so stemmed mostly from anger, while mine was from pure fear. Our last talk hadn't gone so well, and I didn't know that our next would fare much better.

"Do you remember the night of the reunion?" I blurted out, unable to stand the silence any longer. This was a stupid question since I knew for a fact she remembered. We'd talked about it numerous times. But that didn't stop me from asking.

She turned her head toward me, studying me for a second before finally responding with a simple, "Yes."

"When I left you that night, I told you your ex was an idiot because he let you get away. Remember?"

She continued looking out the window, but she replied softly, "I remember everything about that night, Adam."

"Then you'll remember that I was an even bigger idiot."

That got her attention. "What do you mean?"

"It didn't occur to me until this morning, when I was playing our relationship over in my mind that I said that to you, but then I also let you get away. That could've been it. Our story could've ended there." I reached over and grabbed her hand, resting our intertwined fingers on the center console. "There have been a lot of things in my life I wish I could go back and do differently, Carly. A lot of things I would change if I could. But not this." I squeezed her hand. "I'd never change a thing about you and me because, to me, we're perfect. The lives that we'll build. The future we'll have. It's all beautiful and exciting, and I can't wait to start it. To share it all with you. I could've lost you that night, baby. I could've walked out of your apartment and never seen you again. But you found me, at a time when I needed you the most. And I'll be damned if I fuck it up now. I'll be damned if I become an idiot like that douchebag you almost married. Because losing you would be the single greatest tragedy of my life. And I won't let it happen. I can't. So please, Carly, tell me how to fix it."

She gripped my hand tighter, but continued looking out her window. Finally, after a few tense minutes, she turned toward me. "We'll work on it. I think it'll take time to fix it completely. But we'll get there."

I focused my gaze out the windshield. "Don't you believe me? When I tell you that I'd do anything for you, do you think I'm lying?" The vulnerability in my voice angered me. I didn't want to feel that way. Especially not with my wedding the next day. We should've been happy. We deserved to be happy.

"I believe enough of it to become your wife tomorrow," she replied with a slight smile. If it was supposed to be reassuring, it wasn't.

"Is that really how this should be? With you thinking I'm blowing smoke up your ass just so that you'll marry me?" I couldn't help the hardness in my voice.

"I don't think you're blowing smoke. I know you believe everything you said. But believing it and showing it aren't the same thing." She released a sigh. "We have a few things to work on. What couple doesn't? But I'm willing to work on them. For you, I'd work on anything. I just want you, Adam—any way I can get you."

I ran my hand quickly over my face. "You sound like you're settling, like you're making allowances you wouldn't normally make."

She turned in her seat, looking at me intently, clearly wanting me to feel the honesty that would be in her next words. "That's because nothing about what we have together is normal. It's spectacular. I'm not settling for anything." She paused for a moment and rested back in her seat slightly. "I wish I had known."

I turned my head toward her momentarily, my brows knitted together. "Known what?"

She smiled again, and I was taken aback by the genuineness of it. "Known that soul mates were real. Known that you were out in the world, just waiting for me to find you again. I wouldn't have wasted a second of my life with anyone else if I'd known what I could have had with you. This is a bump in the road for us. But we'll get over it. There's no alternative." She simply shrugged. "Without you, I don't even wanna be on the damn road. I'll endure the bumps, as long as I can endure them with you."

She intertwined our fingers more tightly and rested back in her chair, signaling that there was no need for more words.

So I relaxed and decided that, even though we weren't in the best place, I'd still rather be with her than anywhere else.

❤

We arrived at the lodge, and it was exactly as I'd remembered it from when we'd come up a year and a half ago to check it out.

We'd known as soon as we laid eyes on the place that it was where we wanted our wedding to be. The expansive driveway leading up to it curved in an S, flanked on either side by tall evergreen trees. It made the drive up to the lodge seem like you were approaching a castle.

But it was the building itself that had sold me on the place. The architect in me just couldn't resist it. Made of wood and stone, the outside resembled a luxurious log cabin, modernized only by its octagonal shape and the rectangular windows that stretched from the floor to the ceiling. The inside of the wedding facility held a comfortable old-world charm with its numerous fireplaces and wooden beams that spanned across the cathedral ceilings. We both loved the balance that the cozy yet elegant space provided. The bellhop stacked our luggage and carted it inside while Carly and I checked in.

We each had separate rooms for the night, but she'd be joining me in my suite after the wedding. Eva had decided to bunk with my parents for the weekend so she wouldn't have to switch rooms tomorrow. I had already talked to my dad about keeping an eye on her.

Cage was driving up in the morning, and we had offered to let him stay the night in the room Carly would be vacating. That, of course, was before the full force of my contempt for him had reached its zenith, but I didn't feel it would be right to rescind my offer. Though I didn't want Eva getting any ideas. My dad assured me that he'd make sure she slept in her own bed. Alone.

Carly and I boarded the elevator and rode up before we had to go our separate ways with a chaste kiss and the promise of seeing each other in a couple hours at the rehearsal dinner. I watched her get off the elevator on the third floor, holding the doors back from closing so that my eyes could devour her all the way to her room. She turned once and smiled that sexy Carly smile I loved so much. We were going to be just fine.

♥

By a quarter to six, I was dressed and headed downstairs for the rehearsal dinner. It had been an exhausting week, and I would have liked to have taken a nap for an hour or so, but since we had family here—many of whom we hadn't seen in a while—it was nearly impossible to steal a few minutes of relaxation. I stood in the lobby for a few minutes, waiting for Carly since she'd told me she wanted to walk in together. Of course, she'd said that a few days ago, but I hoped it still applied.

When I caught a glimpse of her exiting the elevator, wearing her navy-blue knee-length dress that hugged her waist and showed off the cleavage that peeked out from the low-cut neckline, every part of me perked up. Every. Part. "You look beautiful," I told her with a kiss on her cheek.

"You don't look so bad yourself," she replied playfully as she ran her hands up the front of my dress shirt to feel my chest.

And just like that, the tension between us dissipated and we were back to being Adam and Carly: two people who were madly in love. *Thank Christ.*

Eva, with the best timing *never*, bounded up beside us, overhearing our conversation. She rolled her eyes. But behind her exaggerated show of disgust, I could tell she was truly happy for me. "Will you two get a room already? No one needs to see that."

If only Eva had known how much I wished I could grant

her request. At that point, I would have done anything to get Carly in a room alone. Tomorrow night suddenly seemed years away. "Hey, speaking of things that disgust us, what time's Cage getting here tomorrow?" I asked with a laugh.

Despite trying to remain annoyed, Eva couldn't help but smirk. It was no secret that she loved having a boyfriend, especially one that her father wasn't fond of. It was every daughter's dream. "He should be here by eleven."

"Just so we're clear again, you're staying with your grandparents and never setting a single foot in Cage's room, right?"

"Yes, Dad, for the millionth time."

"All right then," I replied as I led them through the lobby.

Finally, we made our way to the private room of the restaurant where most of the guests were already seated and waiting. The cozy room was just large enough to fit all of us, and the French doors that separated the room from the rest of the restaurant assured me that whatever embarrassing stories were shared wouldn't be heard by the general public.

"There they are," my dad said excitedly. "The groom and his bride-to-be." He gave me a warm hug and then kissed Carly on the cheek.

As we rounded the table, we saw more familiar faces. Two of Carly's bridesmaids—Skylar and Marie—were friends of hers from college. Eva was the third bridesmaid. And Carly's maid of honor was Katie. Carly hugged each of the girls, and tears immediately started to fall when she embraced Katie. Though she had come up the previous weekend for the bachelorette party and spent the majority of the week with Carly, the two didn't get to spend much time with each other because Katie was a junior in college in Florida.

I said hello to some relatives before greeting Frank, Troy, Doug, and my buddy Tom from college. Finally, Carly and I settled into our seats near our parents.

The two waiters assigned to our table filled our water glasses and took drink orders from those who didn't already have them. "I'll take a Sam Adams if you have it," I said after Carly had ordered a glass of wine.

When we'd planned the rehearsal dinner, we hadn't wanted to do anything too formal. And as I looked around at our guests in their dresses and button-down shirts, I was glad we'd decided against a specific agenda for the night so we could all just relax and enjoy the company—just a dinner together with family and friends before the chaos of the wedding day.

The only thing we needed to accomplish was giving the gifts and telling some of the people—especially the kids—what to do. Carly's cousin's four-year-old twins were the flower girl and ring bearer. I knew how difficult raising one child could be, and as I watched Emma and Noah squirm in their seats as their parents struggled to keep them entertained, I couldn't imagine having two of the same age.

The waiters brought out our salads, and the guests easily conversed with one another. "This is nice," Carly said softly to me as she took a sip of her wine. "Everyone together like this."

I brushed a loose strand of hair behind her ear as I thought about how gorgeous she was. "Yeah, but I'll definitely be glad when I can have you all to myself again. Then we can make up properly," I whispered below the surrounding chatter.

Carly's expression changed, and I knew that look immediately: desire. It was good to know I had the same effect on her as she had on me. She squeezed my thigh with the hand she had rested on it, and I jumped slightly in surprise. But she kept it there until the waiter brought out the main course. As soon as she moved it to resume eating, I missed the feel of her hand on me.

"Mmm, this is so good, Adam. Try this," she urged, holding up a bite of her pasta primavera for me.

I let Carly feed me a bite before offering her some of my steak. "Here, you'll like this." I dipped my filet in the peppercorn sauce and hovered it inches away from her mouth. She parted her lips, inviting me to slide the steak inside. Her eyes never leaving mine, she closed her mouth around the fork and let me pull it out slowly. She chewed carefully with her eyes closed, savoring every taste before she swallowed.

The sounds that came from her as she enjoyed the food made me harden further than I already was. It was almost as if she could sense my arousal because she put her hand on my thigh again and worked her way up slowly to stop right below my balls, which were currently pulled up high with an unbearable need for release.

For a moment, I wondered if anyone would notice if she jacked me off under the table. At this point, it would probably take all of about twenty seconds, and if Vince Vaughn could get away with it in *Wedding Crashers*, why couldn't I?

She grazed my stiff cock as she moved her hand out from under the table to take a sip of her drink. And when she swept her wet tongue across her lips to catch a drop of wine that had dripped, I knew I needed to get the hell out of there. "Excuse me for a minute, everyone. I'm just gonna get some fresh air."

"Are you okay, Adam?" my mom asked, concerned.

"Yeah, just a long day. I have a little headache, that's all. I'll be back in a few minutes." I pushed my chair back abruptly, needing to move quickly so my entire family didn't see the real reason I was leaving. And that reason was currently pressed firmly against my pants.

I shoved my hands into my pockets and made my way to the exit, relieved when the cold night air hit me. *One more day. Then you can do whatever you want to her. One more fucking day.* After a few minutes, I got my thoughts—and my dick—under control and headed back inside, just in time to see Carly headed right toward me with a look of confusion on her face.

"What is it? You've been gone for like ten minutes. Are you feeling okay?" She ran a hand along my forehead and cheek like she was trying to see if I felt warm.

"Yeah, sorry. I was just a little ... turned on. I'm okay now."

"You sure?" she asked, her voice holding playful concern.

"Probably not." I sighed with a smile. "You might not want to touch me again 'til tomorrow. I've wanted you all week, and with everything that happened yesterday ... let me just say I have a lot to make up for."

"I think I like the sound of that."

"I'll like the feel of it even better. But for now, I'm begging you, no more touching. I'm not sure how much more of this I can take."

"Guess we'll find out tomorrow night," she replied, hovering her lips just centimeters from mine as she spoke.

I opened my mouth to tell her how unfair that was, but she cut me off before I even had a chance to speak. "Not touching," she whispered, raising her arms up innocently and turning back toward the private room.

I stood still for a few moments, admiring the way her dress fit snugly to her ass, but thinking it was probably just loose enough to hike up around her waist. *This is gonna be a long fuckin' night.*

chapter five

"TEENAGE LOVE AFFAIR" — ALICIA KEYS

I returned to the rehearsal dinner about five minutes later, thankful that everyone was preoccupied with their desserts and paid me little mind. Explaining that I'd been taking deep breaths outside in order to quell the bulge in my pants wasn't exactly a conversation I wanted to have around the dinner table.

Carly sat back in her chair next to me, listening intently to a story her father was telling. It was moments like these that reminded me how well I knew her. Because while her eyes said she was paying close attention to the story, I knew by the tenseness in her shoulders, the fidgeting of her hands, and the crossing and uncrossing of her legs that her mind was on me. Whatever fantasy was running through her head, I wanted in on it. I wanted to bring it to life for her. And tomorrow, I would.

Dinner ended quickly after that, and I walked Carly out into the lobby to say my goodbye. It was only nine o'clock, but we were ready to go our separate ways, knowing that the quicker this day ended, the quicker the next would come. We stood there facing one another, both of our hands intertwined between us, shooting each other shy looks and demure smiles. It was so perfectly innocent, so completely fulfilling. I didn't want to let her go.

"Okay, lovebirds, time to break it up," Katie interrupted. "We all have a big day tomorrow and need a little beauty sleep."

Carly rolled her eyes at her sister before looking back at me. "Guess we have a curfew this evening."

"Guess so." I chuckled.

"Don't give me a hard time. Mom sent me over." Although Katie had propped a hand on her hip, her tone was playful.

"Wouldn't dream of it," I responded before I leaned in to brush a light kiss against Carly's lips. Once we parted, we dropped each other's hands and Katie moved in, wrapping an arm around Carly's shoulders.

Katie was just about to say something when Eva came rushing over with . . . Wait. Was that fucking Cage?

"Dad, um, Cage is here," she muttered, her eyes cast down at the floor.

Yeah, no shit. "I see that he's *here*. The better question is *why* is he here?" My eyes bored into that little dickhead. Though "little" was perhaps an understatement. The kid was nearly as big as I was. My mind again flashed to images of Cage lifting weights in a prison yard while guards with automatic rifles circled him.

"I wanted to make sure I was on time for the wedding. And I was bored without Eva around, so I decided to come up early." Cage shrugged like what he'd just said made perfect sense.

Why are smart girls always attracted to morons? I tried not to draw a parallel to myself, but couldn't help it. Carly was a smart girl. I had been acting like a moron, though I quickly reminded myself that Cage wasn't acting. He really *was* a fucking moron.

"You do realize there's nowhere for you to stay up here though, right?" I spoke slowly, trying to give his feeble mind time to process what I was saying. After a few moments of waiting, it became clear that he still didn't get it. "We only got a room for you for tomorrow night. There's nowhere for you to sleep tonight."

"Can't we see if they have any more rooms?" Eva whined.

I sighed. "They're completely booked, Eva. Not even all of our guests were able to get rooms."

"It's cool. I can just sleep in my car."

I was just about to say what a great idea that was, until Eva gasped as though the idea of her thug boyfriend having to sleep in his piece of shit car was the most horrifying thing she'd ever heard. I wanted to explain that there were much more serious things to be horrified by: like her coming to me and saying that this Vanilla Ice wannabe had gotten her pregnant, for example.

"Can't he have the room he's staying in tomorrow?" Eva cast a sideways glance at Carly, knowing she was asking Carly to give up her room.

Carly and I looked quickly at one another before I responded. "No, Eva. Carly needs that room tonight."

"Why? Can't she stay with Katie?" Eva's eyes were hard, challenging. It was like she was testing Carly to see if she'd come through for her. It was selfish teenage girl bullshit, and I'd had enough of it.

"No, Eva. Everyone is getting ready in that room tomorrow. It's not an option. And quite frankly, it's offensive that you'd even ask that of Carly. Tomorrow is a big day for us.

We don't need to be dealing with this crap."

"It's always all about *her*," Eva muttered. "Come on, Cage. *We'll* figure something out."

I grabbed Eva's bicep lightly as she started to turn away. Cage eyed my hand, and I swear the little fucker growled. I was suddenly overcome with the desire for him to make an aggressive move toward me so I could acquaint his face with the lobby floor. "First of all, fix your tone, Eva. Now. You two are the ones creating the issue here. No one else. So suck it up. Second, *you're* not figuring out anything. You're going up to the room with your grandparents."

"But what about Cage?" Tears were brimming in Eva's eyes, but I was so over all the drama, I couldn't bring myself to care.

"Grab your stuff," I told Cage gruffly. "You can stay on the couch in my room tonight."

Eva's eyes widened, and she looked questioningly at Cage. He gave her a single nod, and she visibly relaxed.

So glad they're amenable to inconveniencing the rest of us. "Go to bed, Eva," I said curtly.

She looked at me sadly, my shortness obviously hurting her feelings. But that was tough shit. She didn't get that the weekend wasn't about her. Any other time, my whole world revolved around Eva, which was how it should be. But not the weekend of my wedding. And I was pissed at her for not recognizing that.

I leaned toward Carly and kissed her cheek. "I'll see you tomorrow. And ... sorry about all that."

She'd been virtually silent throughout the entire exchange, and I realized that it was probably because that's what I'd basically asked her to be: a silent third party in her own family.

I didn't want that, but I didn't know how to make it better.

Eva's behavior clearly showed that she already felt like she was being pushed aside for Carly. How much worse would that become if Carly started taking on a more active mothering role? I was too scared to find out.

"It's fine," Carly replied. "I guess I'll see you tomorrow." She offered me a small smile, one that let me know we'd be okay. Maybe not in the best place we'd ever been, but okay.

"You sure will." I flashed her a full smile, which she returned. I was going to marry this woman tomorrow. I couldn't wait. "Let's go," I muttered to Cage.

He followed me silently as we headed up to our room. Once inside, I told him to make himself comfortable, that I was going to bed.

But before I got to my bedroom door, I heard him. "Uh, Mr. Carter?"

I turned around wearily, having no desire to talk to this juvenile delinquent anymore.

"Thanks," he said simply. "And, I'm sorry. For messing things up."

I released a breath. "It's all right." It wasn't, but I didn't know what else to say to him, so I shot him a quick nod and went to bed.

❤

I'd tossed and turned most of the night, not feeling particularly good with where Carly and I were. I didn't want us to look back on our wedding day with anything but great memories. And I didn't want our wedding to be marred by strain or tension because that didn't represent who Carly and I were as a couple. Our marriage shouldn't start out that way.

The sun rose the next morning over the mountains. I knew this because I watched it. And while I sat looking at the dawn through the large window in my room, I thought about how much Carly would have loved that sunrise. Because it was beautiful...just like her. And that beauty wasn't only skin-deep. It was part of who she was. As the sun's rays hit my face, I finally said out loud what I'd been thinking all night: "I can be a real dick sometimes."

I grabbed my room key off the bedside table and made my way into the living room where Cage was asleep on the pullout sofa. Careful not to wake him, I slowly unbolted the door, opened it, and then slipped out, shutting it softly behind me.

I walked with purpose toward Carly's room. When I got there, I put my ear to the door, trying to listen for signs that she was awake. I heard a menagerie of voices, all talking over one another. *She must be getting ready.*

I knocked, softly at first, but then with more authority when no one answered.

"Coming," a voice said from inside. Suddenly the door flew open, and Katie stood there, starting to talk before she saw me. "Thank God you're here. We're..." She looked stunned as she realized that it was me at the door. "Starving," she finally finished.

"Afraid I'm not going to be much help with that one." I offered her a small smile to let her know I had come in peace. "Is Carly here? I really need to speak with her."

Katie looked over her shoulder and bit her lip. She looked back at me apprehensively. "She's here, but...uh...I dunno. Isn't it bad luck for you to see her or something?"

"Carly and I don't have to worry about that kind of thing. We make our own luck." I smiled more broadly at my words, realizing just how true they really were.

"Okay, well, let me go tell her you're here." She started to shut the door, but stopped before it closed all the way. "I haven't gotten a chance to speak to you since earlier in the week. I just wanted to say I'm really sorry if I caused any problems between you guys. I have such a big mouth." She looked down at the floor as she spoke the last sentence.

"It's okay, Katie. We're fine."

She forced a small smile, letting me know that she didn't quite believe me. She left the door slightly ajar—not enough for me to see inside, but I appreciated that she didn't close it on me.

I stood in the hallway and waited for Carly. It seemed like forever, though it obviously wasn't. I'm not even sure a full minute passed, but it felt like an eternity.

"Adam?"

I heard her voice, but she didn't open the door. "Yeah, it's me."

"What are you doing here? It's bad luck to see me before the wedding." Her voice was worried, but there was a hopeful curiosity mixed in there as well.

"You can keep the door closed. I just needed to talk to you."

"Everything okay?" she asked quietly.

"Absolutely. I just . . . I just wanted to clear up a few things."

She stayed silent, waiting patiently for me to continue.

"I don't want to do it alone anymore," I blurted out. "I want us to be a team. When it comes to everything. There shouldn't be things in our life that I handle or you handle. *We* should handle everything together. I get that now."

"What changed?"

I heard the smile in her voice, and knowing I had put it there was the best feeling in the world.

"Last night...the way Eva reacted...she was that way because I've allowed it. I've created an atmosphere where it's me and Eva and me and you. Like two separate factions. It can't be that way. I get that now. And if you marry me today, I promise that it won't stay that way."

She giggled softly. "I was always going to marry you today, Adam."

I laughed back. "I'm not sure why. I'm really such an asshole."

She laughed loudly in response. "Sometimes. But you're *my* asshole."

My voice grew serious. "Yes, always yours."

We stood there, basking in the silence, allowing our love for one another to fill the gap between us and speak louder than any words ever could. Finally, Carly spoke. "Well, if that will be all, Mr. Carter, I have a wedding to get ready for."

"Oh, trust me, soon-to-be Mrs. Carter. That's far from all."

She giggled again. "I don't doubt it. I love you. See you soon."

"I love you, too," I replied before heading back to my room and waiting anxiously to marry the most wonderful woman I'd ever met.

chapter six

"AMAZED" — LONESTAR

"This is it. Your last chance to just say no." Frank stared at me with mock seriousness as he adjusted his tie and waited for me to reply.

"I'm getting married, not turning down a hit of a joint in seventh grade." My eyes widened as I slowed my words down so that even a dumbass like Frank could understand them. "Trust me, I've given this some thought." All I had done since I'd talked to Carly three hours earlier was think. I thought of the first time we'd had sex after the reunion. I thought about how even then I should have known that she was the one for me. I'd chalked up our instant connection as a purely sexual one, not wanting to acknowledge it at the time for what it was. And I thought of how happy I'd been when she'd come into my life again.

"Okay," Frank said, pulling me out of my daydream. "Just want to make sure you fully realize what you're getting into. You gotta wake up next to her for the rest of your life, man."

Doug laughed and rolled his eyes. Frank had given a

similar speech at Doug's wedding too. I guess he thought that convincing Claire to stay married to his ass for the last ten years had made him an expert on the subject.

"Yeah," I said, knowing he'd hear the sarcasm in my tone. "You say that like it's a *bad* thing. You *have* seen Carly, right?"

"Well, sure, she's hot *now*. But give it a few years. One day you'll roll over and that hot-ass redhead will be replaced with a Medusa look-alike. Not to mention the whole 'no sex as a weapon' thing. Women *love* that. Joke's on them though," Frank added with a laugh. "We can hold out longer than they can."

"We can?" Troy didn't sound so certain.

"Sure," Frank retorted quickly. "Simple anatomy. We can get ourselves off any time we want. I'm pretty sure Vaseline's spike in sales is directly related to the time I let Dylan stay home from school so we could go four-wheeling. I was on the couch for three weeks for that one." He shook his head and cracked open a beer. "Eventually Claire caved like I knew she would. Just proves my point. I could've gone another three weeks."

I raised an eyebrow at the ridiculousness of Frank's theory. "So you think the reason she let you back into the bed was for sex? Tell me you realize that women can get themselves off too."

"Yeah. Okay," Frank laughed incredulously.

"He's serious," Troy said. "How do you not know this?"

"No way Claire does that. She needs a dick to make her happy."

I shook my head as I put my jacket on and took one last look in the mirror. I couldn't suppress my smirk as I adjusted my tie. "You're definitely right about that one, my friend."

♥

My time with the guys had been a welcome distraction from my thoughts about Carly. But now, as I waited at the altar, a strange feeling overtook me. Despite the warmth coming from the fireplace on the side wall, my hands felt cold as they wanted—no, needed—to have Carly's intertwined with them. The seats filled with our family and friends did nothing to make the room feel less cavernous. And the soft overhead lights seemed much too dim for such a celebratory occasion.

As the wedding party made their way down the aisle and I waited for Carly to emerge from the dark wooden door at the back of the room, my fingers tingled with the need to touch her. My breaths deepened as I inhaled the smell of cedar and wondered if she could smell it too. I hoped she could. Something about knowing we shared the same air made the distant feeling seem less lonely. I missed Carly with every cell in my body, and she was only a room away.

And that's when I knew: I felt that way for a reason. The emptiness that consumed me only served to magnify how complete I felt with Carly. It confirmed that we were meant to be together.

Impatiently, I straightened my vest, fidgeted with my tie, and shoved my hands into my pockets before quickly pulling them back out again. My weight shifted from side to side as I struggled to keep my posture confident and straight.

Though the wedding party had proceeded down the aisle, including Eva, I never even registered them. I stood there staring, knowing that Carly's would be the next face I'd see, but no amount of preparation could have prepared me for how beautiful she looked.

Finally, I stilled and my breath hitched as my eyes found hers. And what I saw in them mirrored my own sentiments. Tears threatened to fall from them, and a hint of a soft smile spread across her pink lips, which looked to be wet with the cranberry gloss that I loved to taste. My tongue moved inside my mouth as if practicing for what I planned to do to hers later.

My gaze made its way to her silky red hair, which flowed down past her shoulders. I'd never seen her hair in curls before, but they suited her. I didn't know she could be any more gorgeous than I already knew she was.

I roamed my eyes down her body, focusing on the perfect curves of her breasts and hips. Her strapless dress fit snugly on top and flowed loosely to her feet, and the white satin and subtle sparkle in the beading highlighted Carly's porcelain skin—skin that I ached to lick and caress with an almost unbearable urgency. By the time I'd been able to take in each of Carly's delicate features as I appraised every inch of her from head to toe and back up again, she had nearly reached the altar.

My whole body heated at her proximity as the minister asked Carly's father who'd be giving her away. Until then, I'd been so consumed by Carly, I hadn't even noticed him beside her. Mr. Stanton let go of her, gave her a kiss on the cheek, and guided her toward me. "Take care of her, Adam," he said with a firm handshake.

"Always," I replied simply, before taking Carly's hand in mine. Instantly, with just her touch, I felt full again. I tried to focus on the minister's words, but my hands nearly trembled with how badly I wanted to run them across Carly's body. In the last week, we'd barely gotten any time alone, and seeing her in her wedding dress only served to remind me of how badly I wanted to see her *out* of it.

Finally, I focused when I heard something that spoke to exactly how I felt today. "Marriage is never being lonely or afraid of tomorrow because of the strength you derive from each other here today," the minister said.

I saw in Carly's eyes that she had picked up on it too. All the fear, all the solitude I'd felt for so long, had vanished completely when Carly had come back into my life. I squeezed her hands, tracing small circles on the tops with my thumbs. I knew she loved that—when I massaged more innocent areas of her slowly before moving in to run them down her legs and back up to her most sensitive area. Her expression was full of need, and I guessed my own probably mirrored hers.

The minister's words cut into my sexual daydream, which I hoped I'd get to fulfill sooner rather than later. "Marriage is belonging together through years that are filled with cherished memories, years that are never quite long enough to hold all your tears and joys." Then he looked to Carly and me. "Will you, Adam, have Carly as your lawful wedded partner, to live together in a state of matrimony? Will you love her, honor her, comfort her, and keep her in sickness and in health, and forsaking all others, be true to her as long as you both shall live?"

Without hesitation, I spoke. "I will." I'd been waiting so long to finally say those words. But as much as I'd wanted to *say* them, nothing compared to *hearing* them when Carly said them back.

Both of us smiled. And Carly wiped a tear from her eye before holding her hand out to mine. After we slid the rings on each other's fingers and the minister pronounced us Mr. and Mrs. Adam Carter, I pulled Carly's body against mine, our lips pressing against each other's in a slow, sensual kiss that both of us wished could have been more. "Now that I have you, Mrs. Carter," I whispered against her lips, "I never plan to let you go."

"Mrs. Carter. I could get used to that." She moaned softly against my mouth—a sound that made me semi-erect instantly, regardless of the audience, and I was sure I felt desire radiating from her skin.

The guests cheered and we finally pulled away. Quickly, we made our way hand-in-hand down the aisle toward the door. Pictures were being held in the adjacent room in front of a large stone fireplace. We said hello to some of the guests and headed toward the photographer. Once in the room, it was clear that pictures wouldn't be starting for a while.

The photographer's assistant let us know that group shots would be taken first and we'd have a few minutes to ourselves because he was working on getting everyone rounded up, including Noah and Emma, who were pulling flowers off a nearby table and trying to eat them.

Carly and I moved against a nearby wall, happy to get a little downtime. She leaned into me, scratching my head with her nails as she ran her hand through my hair. "I love you, Adam."

"I love you too, Carly." I placed a chaste kiss on her forehead. "You know what that does to me, though," I said, referring to her nails against my scalp. "And I still have hours before I can take you upstairs." She knew me so well, knew where all the spots were that drove me wild for her. And as she let her other hand drape around my side to squeeze my ass gently, I knew she was doing it on purpose. "If you keep that up, I might not be able to *wait* 'til we get upstairs."

Carly's mouth turned up into a seductive grin. "Is that a promise?"

My cock strained against my pants at her words. "Don't tease me, Mrs. Carter."

"Who said anything about teasing?"

Without even bothering to see how much time we had before pictures began, I gripped Carly's waist tightly and pulled her against my side. "Let's go." I ushered her down a nearby hallway that looked like it had some offices at the other end. *Fuck, at this point, even a utility closet'll do.*

Carly walked with me quickly down the hall, stopping only when I did to turn doorknobs. Finally, I found one unlocked, flung it open, and looked inside. A small kitchen with a wooden table. *Empty, thank God.*

Carly moved toward the doorway, but I stopped her. "Wait." Her eyebrows furrowed in confusion, but she quickly understood when I swept her off her feet and carried her over the threshold. "Might as well do it right." I shrugged.

I kicked the door closed and put Carly down so I could lock it behind me. When I turned around, Carly's hands and mouth were on me, tugging on my belt and rubbing my hard cock through my pants before unzipping them roughly. I returned her aggressiveness, kissing her neck, squeezing her breasts through her dress. I desperately needed a release.

She stumbled backward in her heels as I guided her farther into the room, biting her lip as she moaned into my mouth. "God, Adam. You don't know how much I've been waiting for this."

"Mmm," I growled, "I think I have some idea."

She groaned when her back hit the countertop, and I lifted her swiftly, placing her on the counter. She tangled her hands in my hair and then worked them down to push my pants and boxers just below my ass. My cock sprang free, and it felt heavy with the need to be inside her. I could already feel my orgasm building, and I rubbed the pre-come across my tip. "This is gonna be quick," I said. "But it's gonna be so fucking good."

Her head lolled back in response, allowing me access to the soft flesh of her neck. I could feel her pulse throbbing against her throat as her breathing increased. We were frantic with need, our hands gripping each other's bodies, our tongues colliding with every kiss.

With one arm, I lifted Carly and hiked up her dress with the other. She pulled on the other side of it until it was around her waist. I silently thanked God she'd decided on a dress without a train. I panted against her neck as I put her down on the edge of the counter and yanked her thong to the side. I could feel the slickness on my fingers. With one hand, I gripped the fabric tightly while my other pointed my cock at her slippery entrance and thrust deep inside her with one hard push.

The feeling of her warm, wet pussy around me made me even harder, and she called out as her hips returned their own sensual thrusts. Her nails dug into my skin as she gripped my ass, causing me to pound even deeper inside her. I buried myself in her, giving her all of me at once, over and over again, until I felt like I could explode.

Carly's teeth bit my arm so hard that I could feel it through my jacket. "So . . . good," she cried out. "Make me come. Jesus, Adam, make me come."

I angled my body to stimulate her clit as I rocked against her two more times before she dug her heels into the meat of my ass and yelled my name so loudly that I had to stifle her screams with my hand as I emptied myself inside her, groaning through my own release.

We stayed still for a few moments before I pulled out of her slowly and grabbed a few paper towels. I slid Carly gracefully off the counter to stand, and as I held up my wife's wedding dress and cleaned my come off the insides of her thighs, I hoped that the reception would be quick so I could relive this moment again, allowing myself more time to savor it.

Carly slid her thong down her legs and stepped out of it. "I think you stretched it out." She smirked as she handed it to me. I placed it in the inside of my jacket pocket, loving the thought of Carly without any underwear on. We finished straightening our clothes, and Carly looked at her reflection in the microwave door to fix a few pieces of hair. "Do I look like I just had sex?" she huffed, probably just now realizing that she'd have to take pictures in a few minutes.

"You look . . ." I said as I let my eyes roam down the length of her body, "beautiful."

chapter seven

When we returned to the group, I noticed a few sly glances in our direction, but no one commented on our absence. Well, no one except Frank.

"Hmm, I wonder what's down that hallway?" he asked in a tone laced with faux curiosity as he peered toward the hall Carly and I had just emerged from.

I ignored him, but that didn't dissuade him.

The photographer was organizing the men around Carly when Frank spoke again. "I remember taking pictures at my wedding. I was annoyed because all I wanted was to get Claire alone somewhere. You feel like that, Adam?"

My groomsmen snickered, and Carly's face flushed. I just shook my head and willed the photographer to hurry so I could get away from Frank before I killed him.

After taking nothing short of eight thousand photos, we were guided into a room tucked around the corner from the ballroom. It served as a bridal suite where we would wait until the guests were settled into their seats so we could make our entrance.

Upon entering the room, Frank immediately headed toward a love seat that sat against one wall. He threw himself down and lay back, fidgeting around to try to fit his large frame on it. Then he quickly sat up and shook his head. "Pretty uncomfortable. And definitely not big enough for two people."

Snorts of laughter sounded around us as I glared at him. "Frank?" I waited until he looked at me, ensuring that I had his attention. "One more word and I'll tell Claire you got a stripper's phone number last weekend."

He looked at me, confused for a second. "I didn't get a stripper's number."

"Who do you think Claire is more likely to believe?"

Frank stood and walked toward me until we were inches apart. He looked into my eyes for a few awkwardly long seconds before he said, "Et tu, Brute?"

I didn't point out that his words made absolutely no sense in that situation as I watched him sigh heavily and shuffle off across the room where the rest of the bridal party stood. Doug and Troy both put an arm around him when he reached them, allowing him to keep up his charade of petulance. I rolled my eyes at the morons I'd appointed as my groomsmen before turning my attention back to Carly.

Once our eyes met, we couldn't hold back the laughter anymore. I wrapped an arm around her waist and pulled her to me. She nuzzled her face into my neck, and I had absolutely no desire to ever move from that position.

"Your friends are idiots." She laughed into my neck.

"I know. But they make me seem so much more appealing in comparison."

"Isn't *that* the truth." She placed a soft kiss on my neck before withdrawing slightly to look up at my face. "Thank you," she finally said.

"For what?"

"For being you. For making today the happiest day of my life. For everything."

I didn't know how to respond. Words would never be able to convey how much I loved her—how much I needed her. So I cupped her cheek in my hand and kissed her instead, hoping that would tell her everything I wanted her to know.

♥

We stood outside of the ballroom listening to the emcee announce the wedding party. They walked into the room while the band played an instrumental that I couldn't identify. But once Frank and Katie made their way out, I heard the emcee tell everyone to "Get on your feet."

I looked at Carly. "You ready for this?"

"I was born ready for you, Adam."

I gave her hand a squeeze as the emcee introduced us as Mr. and Mrs. Adam Carter. The doors burst open, and the band erupted into Imagine Dragons' "On Top of the World." Carly and I raised our hands over our heads in that "just married," clichéd way and bopped toward the dance floor.

Carly leaned into me. "Is it bad that I'm glad they introduced me as Mrs. Adam Carter and not Carly Carter?" She laughed. "I had to fall in love with a man whose last name sounds ridiculous with my first." She laughed and I joined her.

The bridal party enveloped us as we all danced to the upbeat song, celebrating the moment with the joy and exuberance it deserved. Once the song ended, our family and friends left the dance floor and found their seats. Carly and

I stayed where we were, waiting for our first dance. And as the band strummed the familiar beat of Edwin McCain's "I Could Not Ask for More," I wrapped my arms around Carly and pulled her flush against me. She brought her arms over the lapels of my jacket and around my neck.

Everyone in the room faded away as I stared at my wife. And I suddenly knew that that was one of the moments the song was talking about. I'd always remember how I felt as I held Carly in my arms: the complete happiness and all-encompassing peace that filled me was nearly too much for me to contain. I felt my eyes moisten with tears I hoped didn't fall. After all, Frank would never let me hear the end of it if I cried at my wedding.

Carly didn't share these same worries and let her tears flow down her cheeks without embarrassment or concern.

God, I love this woman.

The song ended and our guests applauded gently. A server led us to our sweetheart table, and we sat down. I surveyed the room briefly and saw Eva. I hadn't given her much of my time that day, and I felt a pang of guilt for it. I watched the serving staff bustle around delivering salads, and I had an overwhelming need to make it right.

I leaned into Carly and whispered in her ear before beckoning the emcee over to me. I gave him instructions, then stood and made my way to Eva. And as the band began playing "Just the Way You Are" by Bruno Mars, I leaned down to her. "May I have this dance?"

Eva startled and then quickly scanned the room. I knew this might embarrass her, but I didn't really care. She was my Eva, and I needed her to know that that would never change.

She sighed deeply, more to quell the bubbling emotion

than out of annoyance, put her hand in mine, and let me lead her to the dance floor.

She placed one hand on my shoulder as I kept hold of her other one. We began to sway to the music, a little stiffly at first, but then finding a rhythm and moving more fluidly.

"You look beautiful," I told her. And it was the absolute truth. The deep-red dress complemented her porcelain skin. Her hair gathered in loose curls atop her head drew all the attention to her gorgeous face. I had a hard time imagining that I'd had a part in creating something so perfect.

She smiled shyly. "You look pretty great yourself."

"I know I didn't warn you about this dance, but it occurred to me that I hadn't gotten much time with you the past few days. It's been just the two of us for so long, I wanted us to have a moment today that was all ours—just yours and mine. Because no matter how my life changes, the one constant will always be my love for you. And I just..." I took my hand from her waist and used it to tilt her chin up so she was looking at me. "I just want you to know that all my most special moments are only special because you're a part of them. I love you, Eva."

Tears brimmed over her eyes as she threw herself into me, wrapping her arms around me. "I love you too, Daddy."

I spent the rest of the song hugging my daughter on the dance floor, wondering how the hell I'd gotten so lucky.

❤

Once the song ended and the salads had been eaten and cleared, the emcee invited Katie up to give her speech. It was short and sweet, recounting how much Katie looked up to Carly when they were young and how she continued to look up to her as an adult. Carly dabbed her eyes throughout the speech and hugged Katie tightly when she finished.

I watched them, knowing that while Frank's speech might make me cry, it certainly wouldn't be because of how endearing it was. The emcee retrieved the mic from Katie and introduced Frank, who sauntered toward our table like he owned the place. *Fuckin' Frank.*

"Testing, testing...one, two," Frank boomed into the microphone.

I rubbed my face with my hand, leaving it resting over my mouth to refrain from yelling at him in front of my guests.

"Hi, everyone. I'm Frank, Adam's best man."

No shit, Sherlock.

"I've known Adam a long time. Since third grade actually. I know everything there is to know about him." Frank shifted his feet and looked down briefly before bringing his eyes back up to look at the guests. "I'm not always the easiest guy to be friends with. And throughout the years, I rubbed more than my fair share of people the wrong way. But no matter what I did, or what I said, there was always one person who stayed in my corner and who stood up for me when I probably didn't deserve it. And he did that because he's loyal. Because he will protect those dearest to him until his dying breath. Because he's the kind of guy so many of us wish we were. No one deserves happiness like Adam does. And I'm so glad he finally found it with that beautiful woman beside him. You two are perfect for one another. And together, I know you'll live perfectly ever after, because you deserve nothing less. I love you guys. To Adam and Carly," he said as he lifted his glass, prompting everyone else to do the same.

He walked toward me, and I rose to meet him. I hugged

my best friend as I said, "Thanks, man."

He pulled back slightly and smirked. "No problem, pussy."

And just like that, the Frank I knew and loved was back.

♥

The next course was a minestrone soup, followed by that weird sorbet that was supposed to cleanse your palate before the main course. The server had just placed the impromptu dessert in front of us when the emcee announced that it was time for Carly and her father to have their dance. He came to our table to collect her and held her close, much like I had done to Eva earlier, while the band played "Butterfly Kisses" by Bob Carlisle. It was a sweet moment, and I knew that I'd have this moment with my mom right after.

I'd tried to talk her into dancing to Tupac's "Dear Mama," but she didn't think that was very funny. We had ultimately agreed on Lynyrd Skynyrd's "Simple Man." When Carly's dad's song ended and my mom's song began, I thought for the hundredth time that day how lucky I was. And as I slow-danced with the woman who had lost one child and selflessly supported her other when he struggled to finish school and be a single father, I was blown away by how strong she was.

Then she spoke, her voice interrupting my thoughts. "I'm so proud of you, Adam. You've always been such a wonderful father, and I know you'll be an equally wonderful husband."

I looked down at her, and I could see the love in her eyes. "Everything I am is because of you and Dad. If I'm wonderful, it's because you guys taught me to be that way. Thank you, Mom, for always being there. I'd be a very different man if it weren't for you."

She didn't respond, but hugged me tighter until our song ended. I walked her back to her seat before returning to my table.

The rest of dinner passed quickly, and the real party finally got started. The band was awesome, performing covers of popular songs from multiple decades. My eyes stayed on Carly, my hands needing to be on her in some way every second of the night—though it might have been more accurate to say I kept *one* eye on Carly. The other followed Eva and Cage as they cavorted on the dance floor.

I didn't think it was possible for me to hate Eva's boyfriend more than I already did, but I was wrong. As I eyed him in his stylish gray suit with his blond spiky hair, his hands roving all over my teenage daughter, I wished aliens would appear and take him to their home planet. It didn't help that the kid looked like he was in his twenties. *What the hell are they feeding kids nowadays?*

Carly did her best to keep me calm, but when Cage turned Eva around and ground his dick into her ass, I'd had enough. I flew toward them, grabbed Cage by the bicep, and pulled him out into the lobby. I never turned around, though I could pretty much imagine the horrified look Eva was probably wearing. Once we were far enough away that I could be heard clearly over the music, I rounded on that little fucker.

"I'm going to say this one time, and you're damn well going to listen. I didn't invite you to my wedding so that you could disrespect me by grinding all over my daughter. So you either keep it in your fucking pants, or you can get the hell outta here. What's it gonna be?"

Cage was wide-eyed, fear etched on his face.

Good.

"Mr. Carter . . . uh, sir, I . . . I didn't mean to be disrespectful. I apologize for my behavior. I'll, um, I'll . . . I'll keep it in my pants, sir."

I gave him a curt nod before turning around and going back into the ballroom. I walked past Eva, choosing to ignore the glare she shot my way.

"What is your problem?" she asked through a clenched jaw, clearly not content to let my interference go.

I stopped dead in my tracks, turning around slowly in the way fathers do when they want to make it clear their children are in deep shit. "Excuse me?" I took a step back toward her, infiltrating her personal space.

"You heard me. Why are you always giving Cage such a hard time?"

"Are you serious right now? The only people who've been giving anyone a hard time are you and Cage. We've been nothing but accommodating to the two of you."

"Accommodating, my ass. You've been a jerk ever since you met him. I'm sick of it." There was a determined gleam in her eyes, a challenge almost. She wasn't going to back down.

But if she thought I was going to give in to a temper tantrum, then she'd clearly forgotten her toddler years. I hadn't given in then, and I damn sure wasn't giving in now. "Goddamn it, Eva, the world doesn't revolve around you. Today is my *wedding*. So if I want to be a jerk, as you so disrespectfully called me, then I will be. What I *won't* be is tolerant of this princess behavior. You don't like the way I treat your boyfriend? Tough. Time to grow up, Eva. We don't always get what we want in the real world."

My words were harsh, but I didn't regret saying them. They were the truth, and she needed to hear them. I started to turn back toward Carly, but Eva's voice stopped me again.

"That's funny, because it sure seems like *you* always get what you want."

"What is that supposed to mean?" I snapped at her.

"You never even asked me, Dad...if I was okay with any of this," she said, gesturing with her arms. "If I *wanted* any of this. Because what *I* want doesn't matter to you. It's all about what *you* want." Tears began streaming down her cheeks, and I took a step toward her. But just as quickly, she stepped back, turned, and ran.

I hadn't even noticed Cage had come back, but he tried to stop her. "Eva," he said gently.

She simply shrugged him off and kept running. I began moving after her, but felt a strong, sure hand stop me. Carly.

"Let me, Adam."

I simply nodded at her, knowing that to deny her request would undo everything I'd said over the past two days. Watching Carly take off in search of Eva, I found myself left with Cage.

He stuffed his hands in his pockets and looked at the floor. But his eyes didn't remain there long. They quickly found mine. "Mr. Carter, can we talk?"

Why, I'd love nothing more, Cage. "Sure," I replied, gesturing him toward the doors we had just been through not five minutes before. I followed him out and then directed him to a bench off to the left of the ballroom.

He sat heavily, running a hand through his spiky hair.

Deciding that sitting would put me too close to him, I leaned against the wall beside him instead.

"I really care about her, you know?"

His words startled me, but I didn't doubt them. It was in the way he always looked at her, touched her, wanted to stand close to her. It was those things that made me like him less. Because I knew his feelings weren't fleeting. But Eva was sixteen. I didn't want her in a serious relationship. I wanted her to stay a kid.

I forced myself to drop down onto the bench beside him. "I know," I sighed.

"But you still don't like me?" Cage looked me right in the eye as he asked his question, and I had to admit, I respected him for it. The kid had balls, that was for sure.

"It's not that I don't like you as a person. I just... You worry me."

"Why?" he asked.

I shook my head, trying to clear it and get my thoughts straight. "You guys are sixteen. Too young to be so serious. I don't want her giving up things, not getting involved in other activities because she's so wrapped up in you. I don't want anything to hold her back."

"I'd never hold her back. I know how great she is, what a great future she can have. But if you'd ever given me half a chance, you'd see that I have those things too. I'm a good guy, and I want a good future. That's why we're good together. We know that there's life beyond high school. We don't hold each other back. We encourage each other forward. I'd never hurt her, Mr. Carter. I'd never keep her from being the best person she can be. And I'm better too, just because she deserves for me to be."

Well... shit. The little bastard really had a way with words. I put my elbows on my thighs. "You're right. I guess I haven't been fair to you. Your words just show how little I know about you. You're pretty persuasive," I said with a smirk.

"Yeah, well, I have you at a disadvantage. I'm captain of our debate team."

I drew back, shocked. "You're kidding?"

Cage laughed deeply. "Nope, I do all that stuff: National Honor Society, Future Business Leaders of America. I wrestle too."

"God, this is embarrassing. I didn't know any of that. I looked at you and made up my mind without asking you or Eva a single question. I'm sorry for that. Though I will say, the tattoo on your arm doesn't exactly scream studious." I laughed, but in truth, I was trying to justify my assumptions about him.

"Oh, this?" he asked, rolling up the sleeve of his red dress shirt, which I'd just noticed matched Eva's dress damn near perfectly. "This is an airbrushed tattoo. I got it last weekend at a kiosk at the mall. My mom would kill me if I got a real one."

I buried my head in my hands. Then I stood abruptly, turning to face a surprised Cage. I extended my hand to him. He looked at it curiously. "I've been a real asshole. So I was wondering if we could start over. I'm Mr. Carter. It's nice to meet you."

Cage stood and wiped his palm on his pant leg before placing it in mine. "Nice to meet you, Mr. Carter." He smiled broadly.

I clapped him on the shoulder, noticing how solid he was. *It's a good thing I didn't really try to fight him.* "If you'll excuse me, Cage, I think I have some more apologizing to do."

He nodded, still smiling. And I left him to find my girls.

I didn't have to go far. As I approached the room we had been holed up in before the reception, I heard familiar voices.

"Eva, I'm sorry. You were right. We didn't ask if you were okay with us getting married. We were wrong for that."

"No, I shouldn't have said that. I didn't mean it. I love that you're with my dad. You make him happy. He deserves that. I just wish he thought I deserved it too."

I winced when I heard her. *Is that what she thinks? That I don't want her to be happy?*

"You are the most important person in this world to him, Eva. He absolutely wants you to be happy. But you have to see it from his perspective. He's worried that you'll get so caught up in Cage, depend on *him* to make you happy, instead of finding that for yourself." Carly paused, and I could picture how they looked inside the room: sitting close on the couch, Carly's arms around Eva, making her feel safe. Loved. At least that's how Carly's arms always made me feel. "Dads are interesting creatures. They love so fiercely, so completely, that sometimes they become a little blind to what their love can do to their child—how overbearing it can be. But still, it's a special love. One that is absolute and eternal. Once he realizes that he's interfering with you following your own path, he'll back off. The best dads always do. And he is, you know? Your dad is one of the best I've ever seen. So maybe we can cut him a little slack? What do you think?"

I held my breath, worried about Eva's reply.

"He is pretty great, isn't he?" Eva let out a small laugh, and I inhaled sharply.

Carly let out a laugh as well. "Yeah, he really is. And he loves you with all that he has."

"Then I guess I can lighten up on him."

"Good."

I could hear the smile in Carly's voice. I heard rustling and assumed that they were getting up and preparing to leave the room. My eyebrows shot up as I realized I needed to get out of there before they caught me eavesdropping. So I began moving away when Carly's voice stopped me.

"He's not the only one, Eva."

"Not the only one what?" Eva questioned curiously.

"Who loves you. I want . . ." Carly hesitated briefly. "I want you to know that you can always come to me. Because I love you with all I have too."

I heard Carly's dress move again, which I assumed meant they were hugging.

"I love you too, Carly. I'm sorry I messed up your day."

"You didn't mess up anything. This day just got so much better, Eva. You make everything so much better."

That time I did leave. I walked back into the ballroom and waited for my girls. When they entered the room a minute or two later, I watched as their eyes skimmed the crowd, Eva's eyes falling on Cage, Carly's falling on mine.

Both of them gave each other a soft smile before heading toward their men.

"Everything okay?" I asked warily when Carly reached me, though I already knew the answer.

She put her arms around my neck. "Everything's perfect."

I smiled and pulled her in close to me as we started swaying to the music. "Thank you," I whispered against her neck.

"My pleasure."

Dancing with my wife, I gave myself a second to watch Eva and Cage. He walked shyly up to her, a small smile on his lips as he put his arms around her—though keeping a fair amount of distance between them—and resumed dancing with her. He looked up and our eyes locked. I shot him a wink, to which he nodded.

The rest of the night went smoothly. We cut the cake, earning a bunch of jeers when we politely fed it to each other instead of jamming it into each other's faces. Carly threw her bouquet, which was nearly another issue as I watched Eva move to join the other single women.

The thought of some guy sliding Carly's garter up my sixteen-year-old daughter's leg had me pushing people out of my way to stop Eva from making it to the dance floor. But thankfully, my dad was evidently of the same mind I was, because he grabbed Eva's hand and gently pulled her back toward him before she made it out there.

Removing Carly's garter made my dick stiffen, and as I slid my hand up her firm leg, it was all I could do not to haul her out of that room over my shoulder. But I managed and threw it into the crowd of bachelors, not even caring who ended up catching it. And as some guy put the garter on Katie, who'd caught the bouquet, I pulled Carly behind a pillar and pinned her there.

"Can we leave yet?" I asked urgently.

She giggled. "Almost, I think."

"Watching you all night in this dress…knowing that there's nothing under it… If we're not out of here in fifteen minutes, I'm going to hike it up and take you against this pillar."

"Guess we better say our goodbyes then."

"Yes." I ground my erection into her. "We'd better."

❤

Carly and I made our rounds quickly and headed toward the elevators. Once inside, we could barely keep our hands off each other. I pulled on her dress until I could work my hand underneath it to feel how wet she already was for me. "Mmm." I ground against her. "This time I'm going to go slow." I pushed my hips in soft, teasing circles against hers as I pinned her to the wall of the elevator and trailed my lips down her neck to the swell of her breasts.

When the doors opened, we pulled away abruptly and straightened our clothing as an elderly couple entered. They smiled when they saw us. "Congratulations," the man said. "You have a beautiful bride."

"I know it," I said, smiling at Carly, whose cheeks were flushed with a combination of embarrassment and desire. "So what's the secret?" I asked him before the doors opened.

"The secret to what?"

"To staying happily married."

He chuckled before answering and grinned at his wife. "No secret," he replied simply. "You just have to *want* to be happily married."

As we stepped into the hall and the doors closed, I took one look at Carly and I knew there was nothing I wanted more.

We walked briskly toward our room, both eager to start something we hoped would never end. All day I'd thought of how beautiful Carly would look lying naked on the bed, her red hair flowing over the gold comforter as I kissed every inch of her delicate skin.

But that would come later. I had other ideas first. Like I'd done earlier, I swept Carly into my arms and carried her over the threshold. She squealed giddily as she wrapped her arms around my neck. "What are you doing?" she asked as I strolled past the bed and into the bathroom.

I gestured toward the burgundy upholstered bench in the middle of the large bathroom. "Have a seat."

She stared at me questioningly but said nothing. When she seated herself so that her back was to me as she faced the large rectangular mirror, I removed my jacket and tossed it onto the edge of the Jacuzzi tub. Then I loosened my tie until it hung open enough that I could undo the top few buttons of my shirt. She watched my reflection, never taking her eyes off my movements.

I stood behind Carly, my hands on her shoulders before they moved up to remove the few pins that held some of her long curls in place. My fingertips grazed her neck, and I swept her hair to the side so I could whisper in her ear. "Watch us."

We were always able to see the effect we had on the other, but we never got to see how we looked *together*. And I had a feeling it would be fucking beautiful. Carly drew in a few deep breaths as I followed the length of her left arm with my lips until I knelt beside her. I caught her reaction in the mirror when my mouth made it down to her hand and the ring on her finger. "I love you," she whispered, her reflection showing the tears in her eyes.

"And *I* love *you*."

I reached over to dim the overhead lights and began massaging Carly's shoulders—softly at first and then harder until she moaned in response. The sound made my already semi-erect cock stiffen completely. It strained against my pants—a position it had become increasingly accustomed to recently—and I ached for Carly to put her warm hand around it.

Gradually, I slowed the kneading of my hands until I stopped to untie the ribbon on the back of her dress and pulled it loose. Without instruction, Carly rose to let me undress her before turning around to do the same to me. I struggled to calm my racing heart as my eyes followed her shoulder blades and the curves of her hips to her ass in the mirror.

Carly took her time, undoing my shirt one button at a time until she slid it down my arms and let it drop to the floor. Her mouth, only inches from mine, begged to be kissed, but I resisted the temptation. My undershirt was the next to go—this time more roughly as she pulled it over my head. I trailed my fingers softly along her back and tangled them in her hair when finally I moved in to kiss her—our tongues doing the delicate dance that we both knew so well.

She dropped her hands to my belt, and I groaned a sigh of relief as her palm found my dick. I stepped out of my pants and boxers, pulling my shoes and socks off on the way. When I stood back up, Carly's hand returned to my cock, and she shifted to my side so she could watch her hand as she worked me up and down. Her breasts pressed against my arm, and her teeth inflicted a pleasurable pain into my shoulder that I hadn't been expecting.

"I love watching you do that, Carly."

"Mmm, well, I love *doing* it, love seeing your abs harden and your hips thrust toward my hand. I love it when your ass clenches like this," she said, gripping it.

With every word, she brought me closer and closer to letting go, but I desperately tried to hold off, wanting to get her just as close first. Gently, I moved her hand from my cock, missing the warmth immediately. I traced kisses down her chest and lingered on her breasts, licking in soft circles around her nipple before taking one in my mouth and tugging gently with my teeth.

Carly writhed against me, moaning unintelligible words. When she slid a hand down her stomach and began to stroke her clit, I nearly lost it right there. She knew how that drove me nuts—made me want to shove my cock in her so fucking deep until she sheathed me completely. "You know what that does to me, Carly."

"Uh-huh," she muttered. "Why do you think I'm doing it?"

"Mmm, Christ," I growled before lowering myself down between her legs to begin lapping up the juices that had pooled between her thighs. I flicked my tongue sharply against her clit, enjoying the sound of my fingers sliding inside her and the feel of her nails scratching my scalp.

"Jesus, Adam," she huffed. "My legs . . . I can't stand much longer. You're gonna make me come if you don't stop."

I grabbed hold of her ass, thrusting her firmly against my face as I buried myself in her. When I felt her legs weaken even further, I pulled myself away from her pussy to lick up her stomach.

Roughly, I lifted her, inviting her legs to wrap around me as I sat perpendicular on the bench with her on my lap. I played with her breast with my hand and toyed her nipple with my tongue. The combination of watching her head loll back and the feel of her bucking against me had me ready to explode.

"Now, Adam. I want you now."

At her request, I shifted our weight so that I could position my tip at her drenched opening. With her legs dangling at either side of me, she took all of me inside her at once, and the feeling caused me to let out a low groan against her throat.

She rode me hard, grinding her clit against my abdomen. Then every so often, she'd rise up, supporting her own weight, sliding up and down my shaft in quick torturous motions. With every movement up, her pussy clenched around my tip, and then she'd slam down hard, bringing me closer to release.

Our mouths tasted each other's smooth tongues and

salty skin, while our eyes stayed locked on one another in the mirror until it was clear neither one of us could stand to wait any longer.

We struggled to keep our eyes open, to see ourselves locked in such an intimate moment. But when we did, it was nothing short of perfect—to see Carly's face flush from desire, her eyes wide with passion as I clawed at her back and pulled on her hair. I couldn't imagine ever wanting anything else. Carly's body rocked against mine, and I crashed into her three more times before I felt her tense around me. I immediately followed, not able to wait another second before I exploded inside her.

I had been right: it was fucking beautiful.

epilogue

"I can't believe I let you talk me into flying across the country with these two." Carly laughed as she reclined her seat and adjusted her pillow.

"Flying beats driving any day," I said with a shrug. "Could you imagine being cooped up in a car for days on end with two three-year-olds? There aren't enough DVDs in the world to convince me to make *that* drive. That trip would end up like *The Hunger Games*—only *one* of us would come out alive." I shot a terrified look at the twins. "And I have a feeling Nolan and Mya would have a much better shot than we would."

"Nolan, just sit on Mommy's lap and try to rest. We'll be there soon."

Nolan stretched across Carly's lap, kicking the flight attendant in the leg in the process. "Sorry," I said, clearly embarrassed. "Long flight for these two."

She smiled sweetly. "It's no problem, sir. They're cute. How old are they?"

"Can you tell the nice woman how old you are, Mya?"

"Free," Mya said proudly, holding up three fingers.

"Three? That's old," she said with a wink. "What brings you to Oregon?"

"Their older sister's graduating from college. She goes to Portland State."

"Eva!" Nolan yelled directly into Carly's ear.

"Shh," Carly said quietly. "That's her name. They only see her on her breaks from college, so they're pretty excited, as you can imagine."

"Well, I hope you all have a wonderful time in Portland. It's a great city. And congratulations on your daughter's graduation."

"Thank you," Carly replied with a broad smile.

Her words made me smile back. She never bothered to correct anyone that Eva was not her biological daughter. It didn't matter. Eva was her daughter as much as she was mine. Wanting to show Carly how much she meant to me, I leaned over to give her a kiss.

Until Mya shifted on my lap and punched me in the eye.

❤

Thankfully, the night's sleep had been restful. We'd all been exhausted from traveling and the time change, so we'd relaxed in the hotel and just ordered room service. The kids had fallen asleep easily in the bed next to ours, and Carly and I were able to spend some quiet time with each other without the distractions of everyday life.

I didn't even remember falling asleep. I just remember Carly's head resting on my chest as I rubbed her arm lightly with my fingertips.

The next morning we awoke in nearly the same position. It always amazed me how peaceful she looked when she slept— how perfectly beautiful. I gazed toward her, counting her soft breaths, watching her eyelids flutter lightly as she dreamed. Even after all this time with Carly, mornings were still my favorite time of day—a time when I could admire her without any interruptions.

"Why are you staring at me?" She laughed suddenly. I hadn't even known she was awake.

"You know, your eyebrows do the cutest thing when you dream. They scrunch up like you're thinking really hard about something." I brushed some of her dark red hair from her face so I could see how naturally beautiful she was. "What were you dreaming about?"

She ran a hand along my stomach. "You, Adam. Always you."

"Oh, stop. You were not."

She lifted her eyebrows playfully.

"Wait... were you?" I smiled.

She shrugged and hopped up off the bed. "Guess you'll never know," she said with a pat to my thigh. "Now let's get ready. We have a big day."

❤

Several hours later, the four of us were seated and waiting for Eva to graduate. I was thankful the graduation was being held indoors, and I guessed that the typical Portland weather had something to do with that. But an hour and a half later, we were still waiting. *Why do college graduations have to be so long?* Thankfully, we sat on an aisle so Carly and I could take turns walking the twins outside so they could stretch when they got restless. Kids were a great excuse to leave places you didn't want to be: church, family parties, weddings . . . your daughter's graduation.

Not that I was completely opposed to attending these things. They all had their appeal in small doses, but no one wants to hear their uncle tell the same story about the fish he caught off the Gulf coast for the hundredth time. And I had about as much interest in that as I did in seeing hundreds of kids I didn't know graduate.

Finally, they announced the psychology degrees, and I held Nolan and Mya on my lap as Carly snapped pictures of Eva accepting her degree. Until that moment, I hadn't realized just how much she'd grown up. To me, she was still the baby I held against my chest in the middle of the night when she refused to go to sleep. She'd always be the little girl who did cartwheels in the front yard until she got too dizzy to do any more. She'd stay that awkward teenager who didn't care what anyone thought of her.

No matter how old she got, those memories would never fade. And now I had another memory to add to the collection: the intelligent young woman with her whole life ahead of her. I remembered what it was like to feel that way—like your life was full of endless possibilities—if only for a brief moment in time, and I wanted her to make the most of it.

❤

Eva had made reservations for the five of us at a quaint little bistro on the corner of a nearby street. She gave her name to the hostess, who quickly ushered us to a large round wooden table with wrought-iron chairs. I took a minute to observe my surroundings. The restaurant seemed like it fit right into the feel of Portland. Vintage diner signs and license plates hung on the nearby walls, and the large floorboards gave the place a trendy antiquated feel, just like the city itself.

"This place has great milkshakes and chicken-salad sandwiches," Eva said. "They put red grapes in them and serve it on a croissant. The best in town."

"I'll probably go with that then," I said, not bothering to waste time looking at the menu.

"Though the French dip sandwich is pretty good too. That's what I got when Cage and I came here last month during his visit."

I couldn't contain the urge to roll my eyes at the mention of Cage, who thankfully hadn't been able to make it due to his own graduation. It wasn't that I didn't like the kid, but sometimes old habits die hard. I didn't care if he had been accepted to Harvard Law School. He still wasn't good enough for Eva, because honestly no one would *ever* be good enough for my little girl. But even *I* had to admit, Cage was as close as I could see any guy getting.

I had been surprised when their relationship lasted through the four years of college with him at Princeton and her at Portland. But it had, and she seemed happier with each passing year, instead of more bogged down by trying to maintain a long-distance relationship. I also gave them credit that neither of them had sacrificed their own goals to be closer to one another.

The waitress came to take our drink orders, interrupting my thoughts. Carly ordered chocolate milk for the kids, and the rest of us got iced tea and sodas.

We chatted about Eva's final weeks of college: how difficult finals had been, how she'd miss her friends, that sort of thing. When our food arrived, we discussed Portland, which Carly loved. It was definitely a change from Philadelphia. With clean streets, small shops, and friendly people, Portland was much more of a *town* than Philly was. "Other than the rain, I'd love to live here," Carly said.

"Yeah, winter isn't great, but summer here is beautiful. Not as much humidity as the east has, that's for sure. I've spent so much time here, it's gonna be weird having to adjust to a new city all over again."

And with that, the conversation shifted to my least favorite topic: the one that involved Eva moving to Boston to complete her grad work at Tufts University School of Medicine to be with Cage, instead of moving home to be closer to us. Though I couldn't blame her. They were obviously serious about one another, and they'd spent four years apart already.

I understood why she'd made the decision she had. And she definitely wasn't sacrificing her education. Tufts was one of the best medical schools in the country. She'd be able to work nearly anywhere after finishing her psychology degree with them. But that didn't make me feel any better about not having her close.

"Have you found a place to live there yet?" I asked, hoping to sound happier than I felt.

Eva shifted uncomfortably in her seat and started moving food around on her plate. "Um, well, Cage did."

"Well, that's good. But what about you?"

She took a deep breath in and set her fork down abruptly, causing it to clank loudly against her plate. "He found a place for both of us."

I felt my jaw tic instantly. I steepled my hands in front of me and supported my head on top of them. "He found *places* for both of you or *a place* singular?"

Eva held my gaze, showing that she wasn't intimidated. *Good girl.* "He found one place for us to share."

I inhaled deeply, but she interrupted me. "Dad, don't freak out." *How is a father supposed to not freak out when his daughter says those four words?* "We're getting an apartment together. I should've said something sooner, but I wanted to tell you in person."

Deep breaths, Adam. So my daughter's moving in with a guy? A guy she's been with since she was sixteen and who you know very well. Think before you speak, or she'll never come home to visit. "Okay," I said slowly. "Sorry. Just trying to take it all in." I took another deep breath. "You're a grown woman, Eva. You can make your own decisions. I just want to make sure you're doing what's best for *you.* No one else."

"Not even us," Carly interrupted, giving me a sideways glance.

Traitor.

"We obviously miss you like crazy," Carly added emphatically. "But if living with Cage in Boston is what will make you happiest, then that's what you should do." I knew why Carly empathized so strongly with Eva. She had always been independent as well and probably related strongly with Eva's need to be her own woman.

Both of them looked at me, waiting for me to firmly declare my stance. "Okay, okay, I agree." I laughed as I held my hands in front of me. "Man, the two of you looked ready to beat me with your silverware." I grew more serious and turned all my attention to Eva. "I've only ever wanted you to be happy. If Cage is what makes you happy, then I'm happy."

Eva smiled broadly. "Thanks, Daddy."

I was always "Daddy" in those moments—the ones where I completely caved and let her have whatever she wanted. But even though I knew she only said it after shaking me down, my heart still always skipped a beat when I heard it. There was no term of endearment stronger in my mind.

My memory flashed back to one of the last times Eva called me Daddy: at my wedding reception. I remembered yanking a younger, more rebellious-looking Cage out of the ballroom in order to give him a piece of my mind. But really, he'd ended up giving *me* a piece of *his*. I had been impressed with him then, and I was still impressed with him now. Not that I'd ever admit that to anyone.

Eva had definitely chosen a strong, determined man. I hoped I had something to do with that. "Well, at least they have a great program in Boston. Who knows? Maybe ten years from now when you have your own adolescent psychology practice, you can treat these two," I said, gesturing to Nolan and Mya, who had slid under the table and were pulling at my legs. "God knows they're crazy *already*."

"Uh . . . yeah, about that, Dad."

Eva looked to Carly and then back to me. "I actually changed the area of psychology I'm going to study. Well, not *change* as much as *add to*." She was hesitant, which was *not* a good sign.

I couldn't understand why Eva would be so embarrassed to tell me she'd changed her mind about her degree. A graduate degree in any field of psychology would be an accomplishment. "I don't get it. What's the problem?"

Eva's face turned an interesting shade of crimson. "I'm going to school to become a sex therapist, Dad," she blurted out.

I nearly choked on a sip of iced tea and had to take a few moments to catch my breath. *Did I just hear her right?* "A sex therapist? What... what is that exactly?" Again, I looked to Carly, but she only sat there, her chin resting in her hand, clearly entertained.

"It's not what you think, Dad. Sex is an important part of any relationship, and human sexuality is the core of our very being."

Is she for real? Is she seriously talking about sex while we're eating lunch with her three-year-old siblings? "The core of our very being," I repeated in disbelief.

"Many of the traumas we face as children manifest themselves sexually in adulthood. Ultimately, I'd like to combine adolescent psychology with a dual major in human sexuality. It would allow me to help adults recover from the devastating events they experienced as children." When I made no move to speak, she continued. "Dad, it's not like I'll be teaching people how to have sex or something."

"I think it sounds interesting," Carly said, amused.

"Thank you, Carly," Eva replied smugly.

"It's not that it's not interesting. Or worthwhile. I just... Jesus Christ, can we talk about something else?" It wasn't that I didn't want to know what Eva was doing with her life, but I definitely didn't need any more specifics.

"Dad, everyone has sex."

"Yes, I know. But thanks for spelling it out anyway, Eva," I said sarcastically before trying to refrain from hyperventilating. "It's just that when I was sitting there today, watching you graduate from college, I couldn't help but think that you'll always be my little girl." I extended my hand across the table to take Eva's palm in mine. "It's hard to watch you grow up. You'll see one day when you have kids of your own." I shot up straighter. "Although, hopefully that won't be anytime soon."

"Of course not," she assured me. "Dad, I'll never stop being your little girl," she said sweetly. "Even when I'm talking to people about the importance of masturbation."

"Really, Eva?"

"Thought I'd lighten the mood," she said with a laugh.

And for some strange reason, as I looked around the table, I couldn't help but laugh too. I glanced at my loving wife and my two young children, who had picked the moment Eva had mentioned masturbation to finally sit quietly and give their undivided attention to the conversation. And I looked into the eyes of my daughter, who was all grown up but would always be my little girl. *This is it*, I thought. *This is my perfectly ever after. And I wouldn't have it any other way.*

also in the
love lessons series

LOVE LESSONS BOOK ONE

Pieces
OF
Perfect

ELIZABETH
HAYLEY

LOVE LESSONS BOOK TWO

Picking
UP THE
Pieces

ELIZABETH
HAYLEY

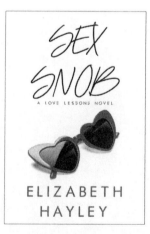

SEX
SNOB
A LOVE LESSONS NOVEL

ELIZABETH
HAYLEY

also by

elizabeth hayley

Love Lessons:
Pieces of Perfect
Picking Up the Pieces
Perfectly Ever After

❤

Sex Snob
(A Love Lessons Novel)

Misadventures:
Misadventures with My Roommate
Misadventures with a Country Boy
Misadventures in a Threesome
Misadventures with a Twin
Misadventures with a Sexpert

acknowledgments

We'll make this short and sweet. Thank you to all of our fans who support us, our writing, and our psychotic antics. We appreciate you more than sex and chocolate, so that should tell you something.

As always, we are extremely grateful to Alison Bliss for her brutal honesty and helpful suggestions. In other words, thanks for telling us when our writing is shit and then giving us perfect ways to fix it.

Amanda, you've always loved Adam, so we hope we did his story justice. Thanks for your continued support, and remember to always protect your voice box in a gun fight.

Lauren, thank you for catching all of our mistakes. You always have your work cut out for you. We appreciate all of the hard work you put into editing our books.

Normally we'd thank each other, but we've run out of things to say to one another at the moment. Thanks for reading!

about

e l i z a b e t h   h a y l e y

Elizabeth Hayley is actually "Elizabeth" and "Hayley," two friends who love reading romance novels to obsessive levels. This mutual love prompted them to put their English degrees to good use by penning their own. The product is *Pieces of Perfect*, their debut novel. They learned a ton about one another through the process, like how they clearly share a brain and have a persistent need to text each other constantly (much to their husbands' chagrin).

They live with their husbands and kids in a Philadelphia suburb. Thankfully, their children are still too young to read their books.

Visit them at AuthorElizabethHayley.com